LONGING FOR THE MINOTAUR

LYONNE RILEY

STORY INTRODUCTION

Valentina has always had a complicated relationship with Banon, the son of the minotaur woman her father married. He's drop dead gorgeous, full of himself, and football runs in his blood. Even though he was instrumental in the misery and bullying that were her high school years, Val has always held a torch for him. Now in college, she thinks she's finally moved on from her childhood crush.

Though he tries to hide it, Banon has hungered after Valentina for too long. She's consumed his every thought for years, even as he put distance between them. When the dam breaks and the truth emerges, will Banon and

Valentina's burning cravings finally erupt into a fire?

CONTENT WARNINGS

May contain spoilers!

- Graphic depictions of sex
- Her father married his mother. You feel me?
- Drinking
- Mention of parental death and parental abandonment in the past
- Public sex

CHAPTER
ONE

VALENTINA

Banon has always been an asshole, and today is no different.

"Tina-a-a-a-a!" he shouts from the window of his car. He still calls me that, even though I've long since switched to "Val." Back in high school, everyone called me "Tiny Tina," including Banon, and it made me hate my own nickname. So I picked a different one.

Valentina is flexible like that, which I'm grateful for now.

One of my college friends cocks an eyebrow, probably wondering why I'm answering to the name "Tina." I wave at her as I head toward Banon's car and open the passenger-side door.

It's messy in here as always, with abandoned Hogburger wrappers and Taco Heaven bags lining the floors. He has a few stupid doohickeys on the dashboard that wobble and wiggle as I shut the door and Banon puts the car in drive.

"Don't call me that here," I snap at him.

"Call you what? By your name?"

"It's *Val*," I enunciate clearly, though I know he knows and he's just trying to get a rise out of me. "Come on, man."

He raises his hands off the steering wheel in surrender. "Sorry, sorry. Old habits die hard. I mean, I've called you Tina since you were twelve."

Don't I know it. That's always what I've been —*Tina-a-a-a!* Just an annoying little stepsister he taunts from a car window. But the thing that's always been most painful?

How gorgeous my jackass stepbrother is. Everyone knows it, including him, which is both part of the reason he's such an asshole, and part of the reason I still let him get away with what he does.

He just looks so pretty doing it.

I'd never tell a soul that, of course. I just nod

along whenever my college friends get a glimpse of him and remark how hot he is.

"Minotaur daddy right there," my friend Natasha said once after Banon dropped me off. I'm just in college and I still live on campus, so I don't have a car of my own.

"Do not call my stepbrother 'daddy,'" I warned her.

"Sorry. Just calling the shots like I see them. He's like four or five years older, right?"

Right. He's always been one hundred percent out of my league, not just because he's way hotter than I am, but also because he's much older.

Well, and other barriers, obviously.

But Natasha was absolutely correct. Banon is big—bigger than big. Fully jacked, and I would know because I've seen how much time he spends at the gym. His fur is buckskin brown, almost more of a gold, with shaggy blondish hair and two big, black horns. His eyes are radiant blue. I could draw him from memory if I had to.

Banon roars away from the curb in that annoying way he always does. I don't even bother to try to correct his driving or ask him to slow down anymore. He won't do it. Well, he will for a few minutes, then get distracted by talking and speed up again, ripping around curves and blowing yellow lights.

I just hang on for dear life and listen as he starts telling me all about his last football practice. He didn't get drafted his last year of college, and now he plays in the minor leagues, trying to get noticed. I think he should have given up after he didn't get drafted, but nobody can tell Banon what to do. He is the definition of a minotaur: stubborn and driven.

In the meantime, though, he works for a moving company, picking up heavy boxes and furniture all day. He's really perfect for it, and he's not the kind of guy who could work an office job where he has to sit in one place all day.

"We still have cheerleaders, you know." His mane puffs up a little. "The squad captain hit on me after the game the other night."

A familiar surge of jealousy rushes through me. I know it's ridiculous, just like every other time Banon's gotten attention from a girl, but I can't help it.

"Good for you," I say, rolling my eyes to disguise how put out I feel.

"Hey, aren't you happy for me? She has a really great ass."

I stick out my tongue. Exactly the opposite of what I wanted to hear.

"Thank you for that image."

Banon grins. "You're welcome. You like girls, don't you?"

I shoot him a glare. "Not girls like that, no. I like nerdy girls. Not girls who jump up and shake their tits for football players."

"Hey, cheerleading is a respectable profession. It requires a lot of athleticism."

Sighing, I gaze out the window. I don't want to hear about his love of cheerleaders. I still remember vividly when he brought home Lillian Esparzo, head cheerleader at our high school, on prom night.

Unconsciously, I shiver all over just remembering it.

"You cold?" Banon asks, reaching for the car's thermostat. When he glances over at me, turning the heat up, there's real concern in his eyes.

"Thanks," is all I say, pulling my cardigan tighter around me.

Surprisingly, the conversation ends, with Banon driving toward our parents' house while I sit silently in the passenger seat, looking out the window.

Tonight is Thanksgiving prep night. Banon's mom, Marissa, likes to go all out for Thanksgiving. It's a really, really big deal to her, and so it's a big deal to Banon and my dad, which then means it's a big deal to me, too. For Thanksgiving prep, we all get together for dinner and talk about what we're going to make on Thanksgiving, draw up a kitchen schedule, and make grocery lists. It's actually very boring, but again, it makes Marissa happy, so it makes Banon and my dad happy. Banon's always been a mama's boy, as much as he pretends like he's not. He'll do just about anything for her, same as my dad does.

And I guess I don't blame them. When the car finally pulls up outside the house, a tall minotaur woman is waiting on the front step. She holds her arms out and I'm pulled into a hug first, where she squeezes me tight as if we haven't seen each other in months. Then she ushers me inside, saying how she made my favorite Jell-O with the fruit inside. I don't really love it all that much, but it makes her happy to prepare it for me, so I never correct her.

My favorite is actually black forest cake with chocolate and cherry.

Dad's waiting in the kitchen, already opening a bottle of wine. Our parents love to imbibe, let's just say that. Wine tasting is their hobby, as is whiskey tasting, and also beer tasting. Dad raises his arms just like Marissa did when she saw me and pulls me into a hug.

"Great to see you, kiddo," he says, squeezing my shoulder and then going back to the wine.

Even though their house is taller and wider inside than most houses, given Marissa's big horns, Banon still fills up every room and hallway he stands in. I have to move out of the way when he comes into the kitchen, and I sigh as he bumps into the overhead shelf he's bumped into every single day since our parents bought this house when I was in eighth grade.

We lived in Banon's mom's house before that. It was a weird situation, all said. Banon's dad had died a few years before, and Marissa was a single mom. My dad and my mom got divorced when I was young, and my dad won full custody of me. It was simple for us to move into Marissa's house when she and my dad got married.

But there were weird echoes of Banon's biological father everywhere you looked—a wall he had repainted, some letters he had scribbled on the wall to mark Banon's height while he was growing up. Eventually, we decided to leave that place completely and find a new home that would be the beginning of our new blended family.

Those were the most miserable years of my life, going through high school in this house. I'm glad I'm in college now, where I've found people like me, people I jibe with. School was never like that for me, not like it was for Banon. Those were his glory years. Mine are yet to come.

Eventually, the wine is opened and poured, and all of us sit at the table to start making plans while the casserole finishes in the oven. It's all very normal. I lift my head to drink from my glass and catch Banon looking at me, his brow furrowed.

I raise an eyebrow in a way that says *what?* He just shrugs and throws back more wine.

He's making the easy stuff, of course, like stuffing and green bean casserole. I'm making the sweet potato pie like I always do, with cream, sugar, cinnamon, pecans, and marshmallows. I'll also be making the gravy, while Dad handles the turkey and the rolls. Marissa is all about the desserts, and she's plotting a lemon meringue and a pecan pie both.

Nobody at our house likes pumpkin pie. It was a huge bonding point between our families: no pumpkin shit at Thanksgiving.

Now that the jobs are assigned, it's time to eat. We've already finished the bottle of wine, so next comes a new craft cocktail that Dad learned how to make from watching a YouTube show. We joke about how well the egg foam pairs with the mac n' cheese, with a side Caesar salad that Marissa threw together so we had some semblance of healthy food in this meal.

"We haven't talked about any of the important stuff yet," Dad says, swishing his cocktail and tasting it again. "Like Tina—I mean, *Val*—I meant to ask how your classes are going."

"They're fine," I say. "I'm glad I switched majors, though. I feel like econ will be a lot more useful to me in the long run."

Banon raises his head. "You're doing econ, too?" He slaps the table. "Carrying on my tradition!"

I knew he'd have this reaction when I switched majors. But going into the humanities had a lot less chance of paying off for me, and with all the student loans I'm taking out, I want this education to get me somewhere after I graduate.

"Yup." I slug back my cocktail. "Going to become a numbers girl."

"Well, I have all the tips and tricks for you.

Especially about the professors. You just have to know what they want to get good grades. I can help you there."

Sometimes I wish we could have afforded me going to an out-of-state school, so I wouldn't feel like I'm getting Banon's hand-me-downs.

"I'm not trying to keep my sports scholarship," I say. "I'm there to learn, and I'm going to get my grades honestly."

For a second, it looks like I've hurt him. "I earned my grades honestly," he says.

"Sure." I look at Dad for support. We've always joked about how Banon is a bit of a muscle head, and in high school, it got him a pass when it came to grades.

"Banon worked hard in college," Dad says instead, a disapproving tone to his voice. "Just like you're doing now."

Marissa gives me a reproachful look, too, and I stare down at my food.

Jeez. I didn't think everyone would get so offended by something I thought was obvious.

Conversation turns to football, and Banon talks about his performance at the last game. He thinks next year he'll move up to captain of the team. I pick my food apart as everyone talks, still feeling guilty, and then getting mad that I feel guilty.

"So, you guys going to stay the night?" Dad asks while Marissa pulls out the Jell-O she made.

Banon chuckles. "Yeah, I probably shouldn't be driving."

Damn it. I didn't think about that when we all started drinking—that I wouldn't make it back to the dorm tonight. I like my roommate, and I like having my own space. My childhood bedroom reminds me too much of my loser years, of the person I was in high school who was tormented by classmates and who had no real friends.

"Fine," I say, scooping myself some Jell-O. I don't speak until I'm done, then I get up from the table, put my plate in the dishwasher, and head down the hallway.

"Going to bed?" Banon calls out.

"Yeah." I don't want to open my mouth and risk further humiliation tonight. "See you in the morning."

Then I'll see if I can get a ride home to campus from Dad or Marissa instead.

Everyone says goodnight, and I duck into my old room, shutting the door firmly behind me. Then I stumble to my bed, my head swimming from all the booze I had tonight, and flop onto it. At least I still have the comforter I like here, and the mattress is definitely nicer than the one I have back at the dorm.

Unfortunately, though, I moved all my sex toys to campus, so I have nothing here to quell the itch that's formed in my lower abdomen. Seeing Banon does this to me, much to my misfortune. I know I shouldn't think of him like this, my own fucking *stepbrother*, but I can't help it.

I push off my pants and toss them aside, then drag my hand down between my legs. It's easy to summon an image that's been imprinted on my mind since I was fourteen.

I heard when Banon and Lillian stumbled into the house on prom night. They had both been drinking—that much was clear by their slurred whispering as they passed my room to get to Banon's. We share a bathroom, our rooms separated by Jack and Jill doors, so it was easy for me to spy on them. All I had to do was push open Banon's door just a hair and peer through.

There, I saw the entire thing. Banon taking off his clothes while Lillian did the same. It was the first time I'd seen my stepbrother completely naked, his thick, immense cock hard and pointing out. Lillian had stroked it a few times before she got to her knees and then sucked him off.

I'd wondered then what he tasted like. Did she enjoy it? I don't personally love giving blowjobs, but she seemed really into it.

And then, Banon had picked her up, carried her to the bed, and laid back on it before ripping open a condom and slipping it on. She climbed atop his lap, took his cock in her small human hands, and guided it inside her.

I remember every single vivid detail, her pussy spread immensely wide around him, his cum dripping down from the condom. His cock glistened in the low light as it moved in and out of her, and though she tried to keep quiet, her cries grew louder and louder.

Oh, how I had wished it was me. I was still a virgin then, but I'd watched enough porn to understand sex.

No porn compared to that moment, though. Seeing Banon thrust his hips up, burying his cock inside her, had nearly undone me.

It's easy to remember it, blotting out Lillian's face and replacing it with my own as I touch myself. My finger speeds up, imagining that thick cock inside *me*, filling me obscenely, driving me closer and closer to the finish line. My hand shakes wildly as I get more riled up, until my orgasm is so close I can almost touch it.

Then, there comes a knock at my door. My hand freezes.

"Tina?" says a quiet voice on the other side.

Banon.

CHAPTER
TWO

VALENTINA

What the fuck is my stepbrother doing at my door? He should be heading to bed too, not wanting to chitchat. We got our chitchatting out in the car, or so I thought.

I quickly hop off the bed, shrug my pants back on, and crack the door just a few inches. I peer out to find Banon there, his muzzle lowered and his cute ears pinned back.

"What is it?" I ask through the small opening.

He tilts his head. "Are you... naked in there?"

"No! I just don't know why you're here at bedtime."

"I wanted to, um, talk about what you said. Tonight."

Great. Just what I wanted—to get raked over the coals again for saying something I thought was obvious to all of us. Banon's never cared about academics, just football. He was open about it in high school.

"Ugh." I widen the gap in the door. "Fine. Say what you have to say."

"Can I come in, please?"

His ears are still down, and I think he's nervous about whatever he wants to tell me. Sighing with annoyance, I take a step back so he can come in. Banon squeezes his big, towering body through the doorway and then, to my surprise, closes the door behind him.

Being alone in my bedroom with Banon with the door closed is something that hasn't happened since I was fifteen and he gave me my first drink of alcohol. Back when he was still living at home, he'd been partying with his college friends earlier and brought back a six-pack to share with me. All it took was two bottles of Smirnoff Ice to do me in. I vaguely remember how, after a few hours of being drunker than a skunk, Banon tucked me into bed and turned off the light before he left with the empty bottles.

Sitting down on my bed, I cross my arms, trying to appear irritated by his unannounced visit rather than elated. If things were different, if our parents weren't married to each other, this would be a much more exciting proposition. As it is, I have to rein myself in and try to play it cool, just like I did my entire adolescent life.

"What's up?" I finally ask when Banon remains standing there, not looking at me.

"Do you really think I phoned it in? In college?"

I resist rolling my eyes. He seems sincere, almost hurt. "Yeah, I do. You got Bs and Cs in school. All you ever seemed to care about was football and women. I don't think we talked about academics once all four years you went to college."

He frowns. "Just because I didn't talk about it doesn't mean I wasn't doing the work."

What does he want from me? An apology? An acknowledgment that he cared a little bit about school but not enough to ever bring it up?

"Okay, fine. You did the work, enough to get passing grades. Good job."

Banon's brows crease, and he lifts his head to

look at me for the first time since he showed up at my door.

"Why do you hate me, Tina?"

The question hits me right in the face. Where's this coming from?

"Who says I hate you?" I ask.

"It seems like you do. All the time. Like right now." He nods at how I'm sitting on the bed. "Your face certainly looks like you ate something gross."

I'm mystified. Of course I don't hate him. I've never hated him. In fact, what I've felt since I was a pre-teen is anything *but* hate. Which has always irritated me more, given how he treats me.

"Hmm," I say sarcastically, "I wonder what could have done that? Maybe when you let your friends make fun of me endlessly. Maybe it's the fact you never once defended me. You just stood there and let them. Remember Tiny Tina? The nerdy girl who wasn't worth the time of day?" My voice is rising the longer I talk, and Banon's blue eyes are getting wider. "Can't imagine why Tiny Tina would hate you, when you were instrumental to the *worst four years of my life*."

I enunciate the last part very clearly. These are all words I've said in my head but never out loud. If he's going to ask me point-blank how I feel about him, I'll give him a point-blank answer.

Banon doesn't speak when I finish. No, he simply stares at me where he stands in the middle of my bedroom, surrounded by posters of my favorite anime characters—the very ones his friends mocked me for drawing during class my freshman year in high school.

"Wow," he says at last. "You've been holding that in all this time? I didn't know you had so much resentment bottled up inside."

"What do you expect? You treated me like dirt, Banon. When you kick a dog, eventually it'll bite you."

He's still staring at me as if this is all new information, which gets under my skin. Does he not have any idea what those four years were like for me? When I got tits in ninth grade, he stood by while his own friends teased me for it. I had no choice in when I got boobs, and never once did my older "brother" protect me.

"So it's about more than just grades," he says, more to himself than to me. "High school was years ago. I graduated before you became a sophomore. Why would you blame me for what happened there?"

Is he really this stupid? "You set the tone. You and your friends, you made me a pariah, and that *never changed*, Banon. When you went to college with a football scholarship, you were everyone's idol. Your legacy lived on long past when you left."

Unsteadily, he sits down at the very edge of the bed, a good three feet away from me. "I didn't know, Tina. I mean, Val. I didn't know that high school was so horrible for you."

"Right. Of course not. It isn't like you ever came home again once you moved out. You just up and forgot about me."

First, Banon appears surprised. Then, his brows lower and he exhales a *huff*.

"I never forgot about you. That's not true at all. Not in the least."

We clearly have very different memories.

"Whatever," I say with a resigned sigh. "I'm sorry I said that thing about your grades, okay? I am." I get up from the bed and head to the door, opening it for him. Sending a clear message to leave.

Banon searches my face, his expression confused, then regretful. I don't know what he's bummed about. All I did was tell him things he already knew. With another huff, he gets to his feet again and comes to the door—but he doesn't step through it. No, he stops in front of me, peering down from his much greater height. Then he lifts his hand like he's about to do something with it but stops halfway.

"Sorry, Val. I didn't know I'd hurt you so much."

I shrug. "I'm over it. We're siblings, we forgive each other and move on, et cetera. Right?"

Something I can't discern flickers in his eyes.

"Sure. Guess so." Taking a step back from me, he turns and strides through the door. The moment he's out in the hall, I close it behind him.

Even after he's gone, though, the air smells like his cologne.

The next morning, Banon is gone before I even wake up, though I thought he'd be the one taking me back to school. That's what my parents believed, too, so Marissa is a bit grumpy that she has to leave early to detour and drop me off.

On the way, she seems a bit sour. I'm almost certain it has to do with what I said last night, and I don't understand why everyone is so mad at me. I'm the one who should be mad. Not that I've ever told Marissa about the stuff that happened at school. It felt like it would be tattling on Banon, creating tension in his relationship with his mother if I was honest with her about the bullying.

Stupid of me. He never deserved that loyalty. I don't know why I afforded it to him when he'd never do the same for me. The one time I had a boyfriend in high school—before the age of sixteen, which Dad had determined was the appropriate age for me to start dating—Banon ratted me out to our parents over dinner. He mentioned "Tina's boyfriend" casually and claimed later that he forgot it was supposed to be a secret.

It had always felt intentional to me.

I'm seething even more than before when I get back to school. Now Marissa is salty with me, when I was just saying what we all know.

The weekend drags by, then it's back to classes. That distracts me from this Banon bullshit, because it's the week before Thanksgiving break and there are midterms to take. I'm doing pretty okay this year, feeling on top of my studies and focused on the work. I got most of my partying out of my system already, and now I'm intent on getting a good summer internship.

Soon though, it's Friday again, which means heading back to my parents' place. They got so insulted last year when I didn't come home for all of the break that I decided I'd join them as soon as class got out, even though I'll be missing a pretty awesome party.

The salt only accumulates as I pack up enough stuff for the whole week, my friends shouting and laughing out in the hallway. That could be me, but instead I'm going to end up having a quiet night in with my boring parents, probably watching a rom-com on Netflix.

Dad's waiting at the curb when I finally leave my dorm, duffel bag and backpack on.

"Stop at the liquor store?" he asks as we drive. "Any preferences on dinner?"

"Whatever is fine with me. Maybe takeout?"

Dad orders a lot more food than we need, but I don't ask questions because I'm always happy to eat it again the next day if it's from the Himalayan place.

When we get back to the house, though, I'm surprised to see Banon's car parked out front. Isn't he going to be off partying somewhere, too? They had a football game today. Surely some cheerleader with a nice ass tempted him into going out.

Great. This is worse than just a night in with my folks. I don't want to face him again after our confrontation last week.

My whole mood deflates as we head inside with the food and champagne. Marissa starts taking out the plates and cutlery, while Banon gets up from the table. He takes the bag from me without asking and starts opening the containers of food.

"Jeez," I say under my breath. I can't even dish up the takeout now?

"Just trying to help," he answers.

Pretending I didn't catch it, I head to the table with my plate full of food.

As expected, Banon talks about the football game, so I can quietly zone out while I eat. Then, as I also expected, we watch a silly movie together. I isolate myself by sitting in the La-Z-Boy, which Banon usually takes during family movie nights, forcing him to sit on the couch that's a little too small.

We haven't exchanged a word or a look. Sure, we've fought lots of times growing up, but it never lasts more than an hour or two before the dynamic goes back to normal. But this bad energy has persisted, and it makes me uncomfortable.

Finally, after the movie ends, the parents head to bed. I grab a book off the shelf and make to do the same thing, but suddenly, Banon's behind me, one of his massive hands landing on my shoulder.

"Hey, Val." He says it quietly, as if he doesn't want our retreating parents to hear him. "Don't go yet? Have a drink with me?"

I grit my teeth and close my eyes. Great. He wants to talk more. But I *don't* want to talk anymore, not with how many ugly feelings that surface inside me when we dredge up the past.

I learned this lesson the other night. Being truly honest with people never leads anywhere good—but I have no real reason to turn him down. We should probably make up before Thanksgiving. I would hate for my whole week off to be polluted by bad stepbrother juju.

"Fine. But you're making me a cocktail. One of Dad's fancy ones."

Banon heads toward the kitchen, sending me a salute. "You got it, toots."

CHAPTER
THREE

VALENTINA

When Banon returns carrying two of Marissa's crystal glasses, each is filled with a pink liquid and a helping of ice. Then he gestures for me to follow him to the stairs, which take us down to the rec room. That's more or less what I call the open space by the old fireplace where we used to play video games and watch TV.

I set up on the couch while he takes up the desk-chair-ball thing we've had since we first moved in. Once upon a time, Marissa had an office down here and used the inflated ball instead of a chair, but then she changed jobs and didn't need it anymore. Now it's just part of the furniture.

Picking up the remote, I'm about to turn on the television when Banon says, "Wait a sec. Try the drink first."

"What, are you trying to roofie me?"

His ears fall back. "Come on, I just think you'll like it."

Something about his behavior tonight is so strange that I can't wrap my head around it. Why, after years of pretending we're happy siblings, is it suddenly like he's trying to make up for being a shithead?

I sample the drink, and it's sweet and tangy on my tongue—but not too sweet, just the right amount. It's got cherry in it, I know that, and maybe some lime to set it off. There's an herbal element, too, that I can't quite place.

"Vodka, cherry cordial, lime juice, a bit of thyme simple syrup that your dad made," Banon supplies.

The cocktail goes down smooth, and I could easily see myself drinking this entire thing in five minutes flat.

"I love cherry," I say, letting out a long breath.

"I know."

My eyes fly up to his. "You do?"

"You always got cherry and chocolate ice cream. Then you had that whole infatuation with Cherry Coke."

"Oh." I don't even know what to make of it. He paid attention to what *flavors* I like? "Wow, thanks."

Taking another sip, I relish it going down. Something about the air feels strange—charged. I lower my glass, and Banon is watching me again, studying me like he thinks I might hold the answer to a question that hasn't been asked.

After a long moment of us simply looking at one another, he sighs and says, "I'm sorry, Val. I'm sorry that how I behaved when you were just a freshman set you up for four miserable years in high school. It doesn't excuse what I did, but I really, truly had no idea how much of a ripple effect it had." His hand tightens around his glass. "I knew it was wrong, letting my friends behave like that. But I..." His breath hitches, and he swallows down what he was about to say.

"You what?" I prompt, because I'm not going to let this go.

"I had my own stuff going on. I didn't want to get involved and... play favorites."

I frown. What? Play favorites?

"I'm your sister!" Suddenly, I'm incensed. "You were *supposed* to protect me, Banon. Not let them make jokes about my tits!"

"You are my *stepsister*," he says in a low voice, and for a second, I think he looks angry.

Oh.

I see. I get it now.

He didn't have to stand up for me because we've never really been family. He didn't want his friends to think he had any bias toward me, and instead I was just some freshman, some trash, the same as all the others.

"So it's like that." I get up and slam my drink down on the coffee table. My eyes are burning. Then I turn around and head to the stairs.

"Tina? I mean, Val?" Banon struggles to get off the ball chair. "Where are you going?"

"If I stay here, I'm going to say things I regret."

"Then say them!" he calls after me. I pause halfway up the steps. "I would rather you say it than storm out and be mad at me all week."

"Fine."

I spin around, glaring down at him—at his stupid big sexy horns, and his stupid big sexy face, and his equally stupid big sexy and extremely toned body, which is pulling at the edges of his T-shirt. My face is on fire, and tears are definitely welling up in my eyes as hard as I try to stop them.

"You want to know? Sometimes, Banon, I do hate you. I hate that you left for college and didn't come back. I hate that you sleep with these bimbos all the time, and I worry that you're gonna get an STI. And I really hate that you've always kept me at arm's length, like we were never really part of the same family."

He opens his mouth like he's going to deny it, but then he grits his teeth and looks down.

"You're right." Both his hands curl into fists. "I have always put a distance between us."

Somehow, it doesn't feel as good as I was hoping or expecting, that he would say this. That he would agree with me.

I turn around fully, lowering myself to sit on the stairs. "Why?" The tears I've been holding back finally break free. "Why wasn't I good enough for you?"

His brows rise to his hairline. He approaches me on the steps, kneeling a few down so we're almost at eye level.

"It's not that," he says, his voice turning to a whisper. "It's that you're *too* good for me. You were always so soft and innocent. Sweet and naive. I shouldn't have gotten you drunk that one time. I regretted it a lot."

Now it's my turn to be perplexed. "What? That was the best night ever. It was the only time I felt like we... like we were friends."

There. I said it.

Banon lowers his head, ears drooping. Even his tail falls to the carpet.

"I corrupted you. You were so young, I shouldn't have."

I want to tell him no, that didn't corrupt me. What corrupted me was seeing him fuck Lillian Esparzo on prom night, his thick cock gliding in and out of her while she tried not to make noise.

"And why not?" I ask. "That's what older siblings are supposed to do. Corrupt. Show us things about the world."

"We aren't siblings!" Abruptly, Banon stands up. His mane rises and his fur bristles. "We aren't related, Tina. That's what I've been trying to tell you. I..." He slams his mouth closed, so hard I can hear his teeth chatter.

Here we are again. The truth.

"I'll never really be family to you." It hurts just to say it out loud. "I get it."

I rise to my feet. Banon follows me with his

eyes but doesn't deny it. Then I turn around and go the rest of the way up the stairs.

He doesn't follow me.

The rest of the weekend is miserable. Banon and I studiously avoid each other. Our parents shoot us odd looks when there's silence over the dinner table. On Monday, Banon goes home, even though he said he was going to stay for the whole week.

He doesn't come back.

One night, I'm sitting on the porch in my big coat and texting with one of my friends from school, who's also gone back home for the break, when the sliding glass door opens. Marissa steps out, wearing her coat, and sits down on the porch beside me.

I put away my phone to be polite.

"What's going on, girl?" she says in that voice she uses when she's trying to be hip with me. "Talk to me."

"About what?" I'm not sure where she's going with this.

"What happened with Banon? Clearly something did. You two haven't spoken a word to each other, and then he went home."

Ugh. I knew this was going to come up eventually when he peaced out for the week.

"It's nothing. Just... hashing out old stuff."

"What kind of old stuff?"

I grumble. I don't want to open this wound again.

"Just about back in high school. He wasn't really great to me, you know."

"He was a bit full of himself." She cocks her head. "Not as much now, though."

Little does she know, I'm still nothing to him.

"Yeah, all right," I say, noncommittal.

A pregnant silence passes between us as I fiddle with my phone in my pocket.

"You know, I met Banon's father in a really unusual way," Marissa finally says. "He was my bully in grade school."

"What? You married your *bully*?"

She nods, rubbing her cheek. "Yep. He was so mean to me because, well, he liked me and didn't know how else to show it. And he didn't want the other kids to notice he had a crush, so he was extra mean to me." She chuckles. "We met again not long after I graduated college. We were both in line at the DMV. The first thing he did was apologize to me."

"Wow. I guess you forgave him, huh?"

"I mean, he was a kid at the time."

"True," I say. "I'm glad you had him while you could."

I don't really know what this has to do with my situation, though. Unless she knows that...

No, I don't think so. I've always kept hidden very carefully how I feel about Banon. If I outed myself, that could do terrible things to my family.

Marissa pats my back. "Me too. Anyway, I hope maybe you can forgive that idiot kid of mine for what he did when he was younger. It's not representative of who he is now."

I don't want to tell her that just last night he told me we weren't family. That we've never had that. That we're just strangers bound together by our parents' marriage.

"Okay," I say with a shrug. Marissa pats me on the shoulder.

"Want some leftover pie?"

CHAPTER
FOUR

BANON

Fuck. God damn it.

I really need to go back to the folks' house. I took all of Thanksgiving week off work, which was pretty hard to negotiate, and now I'm spending it at my apartment alone. Rich has gone back to Minnesota to see his own family, so it's just me here, eating pizza and then leftover pizza, then making mac 'n' cheese from a box and eating leftover mac 'n' cheese from a box.

But I don't want to go back. Seeing Tina's face again after how we left it would ruin me.

I know I hurt her, but I'm just trying to get her to *see*. If only she knew how I felt about her, she wouldn't insist that we're family. If she knew even half the things I think about her, she would never look at me the same way again.

I can't have that. We're hanging on by a thread, and even that thread is fraying the longer I stay away.

Finally, it's Thanksgiving morning, and I'm out of excuses. I have to go to the house and face her after what I said, what she surely thinks I meant.

I take a long shower, where I think only about Tina, about her tiny waist and perfect hips, her big, bouncy tits and adorable smile. It's true, she doesn't smile as often now as she did when she was younger. I wonder how much high school wore her down in my absence.

That slows my hand down where I've been stroking myself under the hot water. I really didn't know what they were doing to her in my name. When I was in college... well, I was getting as far away from Tina as possible.

Yeah. I didn't visit. I was nineteen and had a thing for my fifteen-year-old stepsister. It was fucked up, and I knew I needed to keep my distance. Let her be herself without my influence, try to disentangle myself as much as I could.

In the meantime, I left her to the wolves that are high school students. Yeah, I was getting pussy at the time, and lots of it. But that was so I could fucking *forget* about her.

I speed up my strokes again, running my hand over my cock from the thick root to the blunt tip. How many times have I imagined Tina in her swimsuit on our Cancún trip last year, where she was playing in the water like a dolphin?

Dozens of times, the sick fuck that I am.

After my shower, I finish my energy drink and pick up the bag of groceries Mom instructed me to bring, then head out to the car.

When I arrive, Mom and Fred both hold up their arms and hug me. Fred's a good guy, truly. I'm happy Mom found him after losing my dad. But Fred isn't *my* dad and never will be.

Tina—I mean, Val, I really am trying to get it right—stands off to one side, scrolling on her phone. She doesn't even look up when I come in.

"I'm going to start on the sweet potato pie now, Marissa," she calls out as she heads to the kitchen. "Get the prep out of the way so that it's just ready to go in and cook later."

"All right, honey!" Mom calls after her, and I cringe at the endearment. But then my mother grabs me by the hand and tugs me off to one side of the door while Fred heads after his daughter.

"Banon," she says in a strict tone, "whatever you said to Valentina, I want you to apologize."

I gape at my mom. What does she know? What did Val say?

"I have nothing to—"

"It's not my business," she says quickly. "But the two of you aren't going to ruin Thanksgiving by being all pouty and fighting. I need you to patch things up with Val before dinner. Do you get me?"

My mom is usually a pretty nice, easygoing minotaur. Usually. Not so much when it comes to Thanksgiving, I guess.

"All right, I get you," I say, rubbing my horn. "I'll figure it out."

"That's my boy." She ruffles my hair as if I'm still five years old. "Maybe go for a walk with her and sort it out."

Of course, she thinks a nice walk is the answer to everything.

It's only a few minutes later that Mom says, "Oh, gosh, I forgot condensed milk." She turns to me. "Banon, will you please go down to the store and get some?"

I see her cue and sigh. "Fine."

"And Val, honey?"

Val looks up from her phone. "What is it?"

"Go with him, will you? Make sure he doesn't buy Gummi Worms, and that he comes back with the right brand."

Tina groans, as if she couldn't be more obvious that she'd rather do anything besides walk to the store with me.

"Fine," she says, already heading over to the doorway to grab her coat. She shoots me a glare. "You coming?"

Quickly I get my own coat, then head out after her.

We walk in silence for the first few blocks, even though I know I need to break it and say something. But what? I don't take back what I said the other night. I just could have phrased it better.

"I'm sorry about the other night," I finally say. "I didn't mean to hurt you."

"Maybe you didn't, but you said what was true to you."

She doesn't look up as she says it. Her shoulders are slumped, like she's resigned.

I kick a rock. I despise that she feels this way, when I'm the one who caused it.

"Just because you aren't my blood sister doesn't mean that I don't... that I don't see you as someone close to me. As my friend."

Instead of heading down the busy streets, I lead us more out of the way, through the park. There's almost nobody out and about on Thanksgiving—the path is completely empty.

"I've never gotten that impression," she says dryly.

I don't want to fight with her today. "It's true. I've always cared about you a lot."

"Whatever you say."

We fall silent again as we keep walking, deeper into the park. There are a few benches here and there, with a wide green space for dogs to play in and people to lie on blankets and read.

Sometimes I've wondered what it would be like to have that life with Val. To lie on the grass with her and read our books, her head resting on my chest, my hand tangled in her hair.

Something normal. Something where I didn't have to always hide, always try to pretend like I don't crave her, like I don't want to eat her and absorb her inside myself and never let her go again.

I think that maybe it's slowly killing me. Every moment that passes where she hates me, where she thinks I don't love her the way I do, is grinding my bones into a fine dust.

And it may never stop eating me alive unless I do something about it. She will probably react with horror, with disgust. She might even tell our parents. But what else can I do? I don't want to spend the rest of my life regretting what things could be like if I'd not been such a coward.

Whatever the ramifications are, it's better than Val believing I hate her forever. I don't know that I could bear it.

"Val." I pause in front of one of the park benches. "Can we, um, sit?"

She glares at me. "We're going to get condensed milk. Marissa needs it, and there's a lot of cooking to do today. I didn't even start on the sweet potato—"

"Please." I hold out my hand to her, and she appears confused by it. Slowly, while I wait, she extends her own hand and sets it in my palm. I wrap my fingers around it, using it to pull her in closer. Finally, she succumbs and sits down on the bench beside me.

"What is it?" she says with a tired sigh. "We've hashed this out already. Twice."

"Valentina," I say, my voice traveling over every syllable of her full name carefully, testing it. "I should call you that more often."

She blinks up at me, perplexed. "Why?"

"Because it's a beautiful name."

I have to tell her. Fuck, I have to, but it's hard. It's so impossibly hard to break this barrier between us—the one I made, the one society has constructed around us. It feels utterly idiotic to ruin things even more with her, when it could have such disastrous ramifications for our family.

And yet. Even if she doesn't share my feelings, which I doubt she does after all she's been through, maybe I can explain to her why I have to push her away, why I have to distance myself from her to keep everyone safe.

Val squints. "You've known my name for years. You're just now noticing?"

"I've loved it ever since I first learned it."

"Then why did you make fun of it?"

Here it goes.

"Because I had to throw them off the scent," I say, bracing myself. "I didn't want everyone else to know that I liked you."

I'm still holding onto her hand, but she pulls it away.

"What? You mean, liked me as a friend, right?"

"No." I stare right into her brown eyes as I speak the words into existence. "I have never seen you as my sister. I've never seen you as just a friend, either. Though there's that, too."

"Yeah, we covered this last night," Val says, bringing her coat in tighter around herself as she pulls away from me.

I gnash my teeth together, trying to muster what it takes to do this.

"You don't get it!" I need her to really listen to me. "Do you remember when we all went to Cancún for Christmas break?"

She arches an eyebrow. "Yeah."

"I couldn't stop staring at you. Couldn't fucking stop it. In that cute little bikini? I think about it every night, Valentina. I remember how you looked in it better than I know the back of my own hand. And how much I just wanted to tear it off you? Painful."

I can see the moment that understanding dawns on her, but I barrel forward anyway.

"This is why you will never be my sister. Because I..." I breathe through it, even though Val sits in shocked silence. "Because I love your voice, your brain, your tits, everything. I love how you put people in their place. I love how you know your own worth. And I—"

I finally choke, because now I'm at the extra fucked-up part. The part I'm terrified of. Val is stricken, and I'm even more terrified of what she's going to say once I squeeze out this last vial of bloody truth.

"I *want* you," I manage, my voice rough and low and raspy. "I want you so, so bad. I've wanted you for years. It's why I tried to escape you. Why I didn't come home."

All I see when I look at her is shock and confusion.

"Damn it," she says, her breath speeding up, her expression turning furious.

I've ruined everything. I have literally dropped a bomb on our lives. And for what?

"Are you serious?" she asks, peering up at me with eyes like knives. "Are you pulling my fucking leg, Banon? I don't know why you would, but..."

It breaks my heart that she thinks I would make this up just to screw with her.

"I'm telling you the truth, the real truth. This is the monster that's been locked up inside me all this time." My heart is racing in my chest, ready to burst out of me like a goddamned alien.

"I know I'm disgusting. And I'm sorry. I'm sorry for every stupid thing I did trying to prove that it wasn't true. Trying to prove to *myself* that I wasn't fucking obsessed with you."

Val doesn't speak at all as her eyes fall to the ground. She's horrified, as I expected.

"Fuck!" I run my fingers through my hair. "Fuck, I am so sorry. I shouldn't have said any of this, I—"

"Shut up." She grabs my hand in hers and squeezes it hard. "Just stop."

So I do. I listen and I stop moving, stop talking, stop breathing.

"Thank you," she says. "Thank you for finally telling me."

My heart spasms. Is she going to forgive me? I know that's too much to ask, but I can hope.

"I understand so much more. And that, I'm really, really grateful for." Finally, she looks up at me again. "Why did you out me and Cory?"

Huh? My brain stutters to a halt.

"Cory?" I ask. "Who the fuck is that?"

"My boyfriend. When I was a freshman."

Right. Cory, that skinny guy who was always trying to get in with the football players. He thought being a filthy-mouthed jackass was the way into the cool-kids crowd, and he said some things about Valentina he regretted when I beat him to a pulp later.

"Because I couldn't stand him," I growl. "Because he didn't deserve you." I lean down closer to her, still holding her hand, clasping it tighter as my lips reach her ear. "Only I do."

CHAPTER
FIVE

VALENTINA

Never in my life have I been so supremely taken off-guard. The very last thing I expected Banon to say was that he lusted after me in a bikini. And my voice? Who notices somebody's voice?

I can feel Banon's heavy breaths against the shell of my ear, and it sends a shiver down my arms. Instantly, my body is awake, remembering every last dirty thought I've ever had about him.

Dirty thoughts that *he* has apparently also had about *me*.

If I hadn't seen the pained expression on his face as he told me, I would never believe what he just said. I can't help but feel like Banon's messing with me, somehow. Am I going to wake up and this will all be a dream? Is it an elaborate joke and I'm walking right into it?

He tattled on me having a boyfriend because he was jealous. That makes it sting far less.

Banon holds my hand, perilously close, the scent of his cologne filling my nose. He's worn the same one since high school, and it still does unspeakable things to me. My body is warm all over, so warm that I don't even notice the cold breeze picking up.

"I was fifteen when you left home," I say slowly, still trying to understand.

Banon exhales. "I know. Fucked up. So fucked up. That's why I had to go."

That makes so much more sense now, too. It's not how I would've gone about it, but at least I understand.

"Hey." I lean back so we can look at each other. It's always been wonderful to me how in-human his face is, with his long muzzle and broad nostrils and wide-set eyes. "You don't have to be ashamed. With me. Of how you feel."

He inhales sharply. "Really? You're not... horrified?"

How could I be, when I've had the same

thoughts ever since I met him? That first time I was introduced to Dad's new girlfriend and her teenage son, I was a goner.

"Well, would it be even more horrible of me if I said that I get it?" I wrap both my hands around his. "That I've felt the same way since the day our parents got married?"

His jaw flexes. "It wouldn't be horrible, no," he says, voice strained. "Not at all."

"Then what you feel isn't horrible, either."

Banon doesn't look like he believes me. "You can't be serious."

I guess it's time. He's bared his soul to me, told me the truth he's been hiding all along, and now I should do the same—take a leap, hoping it's the right one.

"Dead serious. I couldn't take my eyes off you on that Cancún trip, either." I bite my lip, thinking of the moment that changed my life forever. "And... I saw you. Once. With Lillian. Back in high school."

His brow wrinkles. "What do you mean, with Lillian?"

"Prom night. You brought her home." I swallow hard as I stare my shame right in the face. "I peeked."

His eyes get huge. "You saw me fuck Lillian?"

I nod.

"Fuuuuuck." He rubs his face. "You should never have seen that. No, no, no." He drops his head into his hands, and I worry I've severely messed up.

"What's wrong?"

"I don't want you to even think about that!" He sits up abruptly and glares down at me. "Don't ever, ever think about that, Valentina. That wasn't about her, not ever."

"How could it not be?" I ask. "You were… inside her."

Banon groans miserably. "Yeah, I was. Fuck. I was. But…" He turns his head away, like he can't look me in the eyes as he says what comes next. "It was always about you. About how much I wanted you. I've only slept with other women because I can't have *you*!"

Words I could have never dreamed of, never imagined. Words that ripple through me, from my chest down to the emptiness between my legs.

Banon. The minotaur jock who's been the subject of my fantasies for years, wants me.

Suddenly, I don't just want to kiss him. I want to get on his lap and give us what we both want, what we both deserve. I need him to wrap those arms around me and tell me this all over again, that it's for real and I don't have to hide from how I feel anymore.

I want to know him. To learn him, without this wall between us. And then I want more, and more, and even more than that.

"I won't ever think about it again," I whisper to him, raising my hand to brush along his cheek. "If you give me something else to think about instead."

His breath hitches. "You don't mean—"

"I do mean."

Banon licks his lips, his eyes homing in on me. With his other hand, the one not trapped by mine, he skims down my shoulder to my side, then over my hip. There, he stops and grasps it tight.

"You don't have any fucking idea what you do to me, do you?" He tilts his head. "No clue. This whole time."

I shake my head, unable to utter a word.

"You make me crazy." He shifts me closer to him, his neck bending further down so our faces are very close together. "And you felt the same way. All this time."

His mouth is dangerously close to mine now.

If we do this, we can't go back. There's no re-versing it.

"All this time," I agree.

When he finally kisses me, it's rough. It's rough and demanding and so ravenous that all I can do is cling onto him and go along for the ride.

I've never been kissed like this, as if he's everywhere, surrounding me. He's invading my mouth with years of pent-up need and unleashing all of it at once. I feel the dam break, too, and then I'm practically in his lap, our hands all over each other, our lips moving in a sensual, messy rhythm. He's pulsing under me, his fingers every-where, tracing the outline of my tits, the curve of my hips, cupping my ass. They dig in, squeezing me, and his mouth grows even more urgent and insistent. His hips buck up into me, and under my hands, I can feel his heart racing as fast as mine.

"Valentina," he moans, and the sound of my name in that throaty, lusty voice makes me want to rip off my clothes and do unspeakable things to him. But we're in public—in a park, no less—and we have things to do or the parents will get suspicious.

Reluctantly, I pull away, and we're both

gasping for air. Then Banon grabs my face in his hands and brings me in again, whirling me into a bruising kiss. Finally, he releases me, and he's hard as a rock under his jeans.

"Heh," he says as I stand up, and he follows me. His erection is tenting his pants in a noticeable manner. "You should walk in front of me for a while. So I can admire your ass."

Hearing those words in Banon's voice does something to me. My thighs clench, but I try to ignore it as we resume walking down the path. After a few minutes, he takes up step beside me again, and it looks like he's mostly returned to normal.

I'm most surprised when he scoops up my hand in his much larger one, twining our fingers together. When I glance up, he's smiling down at me, and now I don't have to wonder anymore what it would feel like if he smiled at me that way.

When we get back home, it's all hands on deck getting ready for Thanksgiving. We're all in each other's way, despite how we prepared and scheduled, because our little side quest took some time.

Banon finds an opportunity to glance his hand over my ass as we pass each other by the sink, and I nearly jump out of my skin. He winks as he goes by with the container of flour.

We take breaks while things cook, snacking on vegetables and ranch dressing. Marissa turns on some holiday music, and we take turns dancing along with it. Dad takes Marissa by the hand and twirls her around, making her giggle.

Banon glances at me like he would if he could.

Soon, the alcohol comes out, and the turkey gets closer to finishing. Everyone is in a good mood. Whenever I look over at Banon, he's already got his eyes on me, watching like he wants to eat me even more than Thanksgiving dinner.

Finally, the oven timer beeps, and the turkey comes out. Banon whips together the gravy while the last few items come off the stove, and we plate everything up and bring it to the table.

"Thanks for pitching in, everyone," Dad says, raising his glass of wine. "This year, I'm grateful for my kids, who always find time to spend with their folks even though they have lives of their own. Cheers to another year."

We all hold up our drinks and clink them together. Then, we dig into the food.

I've always loved Thanksgiving, as problematic as it is. Each year, I try to take a moment and reflect on what I'm truly grateful for.

Under the table, a foot nudges mine, and when I glance up, Banon's smirking at me.

"Valentina," he says in a silky voice, "pass me the gravy?"

Marissa nods approvingly, clearly pleased that we've made up.

I stuff myself so full I almost don't have room for the amazing pie that's been cooking, but I manage. There's always room for pie.

After we've all worked together to clean up and put away the leftovers, Marissa yawns dramatically.

"I'm exhausted, Fred," she says to my dad. "Can you wrap up out here?"

He nods and kisses her on the nose before she retreats down the hall. I find myself pretty exhausted, too, so after finishing off my wine, I get the dishwasher going and say goodnight.

"Goodnight, sweetie," Dad says, giving me a hug.

Banon nods at me with a grin, his eyes twinkling. "Goodnight, Val."

I smile back, and for the first time since I was a girl, I feel like I finally understand him. Like the pieces of the puzzle that is our lives makes sense.

I wave as I head off to my room. "Goodnight."

I'm reclined on my bed in my pajamas, reading a book I swiped off Marissa's shelf, when I hear the slightest, lightest knock at my door.

It must be Banon.

I open it quietly, and sure enough, there's an immense, handsome minotaur standing on the other side.

"Can I come in?" he whispers.

My entire body lights on fire at once.

"Yes," I say, opening it for him. "Please do."

In the blink of an eye, he pushes the door closed with one hoof, then descends on me. His arms curl around my back, dragging me in close as he kisses me again. This time, he's gentler, more exploratory, but his hands are another story. One ducks under my shirt while the other slides down my ass to cup it. With our hips pressed so close together, I sense when he grows hard under his jeans again, and I want nothing more than to set him free.

"Valentina," he murmurs against my lips, gently pushing me toward my bed. "Do you know how to be quiet?"

I nearly choke. So he wants the same thing I do. Right now.

"I know how to be quiet."

Little does he know I've had quite a bit of dorm sex, trying to keep it down so I don't wake the girls that share a thin wall with me.

"Good," Banon says, his blue eyes burning. "Because I'm going to make you want to scream."

CHAPTER
SIX

Picking me up easily with both hands, Banon sets me down on the edge of the bed. His gaze roams over me, a broad grin spreading across his face.

"You're so fucking gorgeous. I can't believe how long I've wanted to tell you that." He traces my jaw with his index finger. "Just so damned beautiful. Like the entire universe was waiting for you to appear."

I'm panting now as he leans over me on the bed. Banon dips his hand under the hem of my shirt.

"You know what I've needed more than anything?" he asks.

I shake my head, not trusting my own voice.

"To see you."

He pulls my shirt up over my head and soon, it's gone, leaving me topless. I feel so exposed to him like this, my huge tits out for his judgment. His eyes are fastened to my nipples, and he drags a palm down his crotch, over the long bulge there.

"Damn," he murmurs, resting one of his haunches on the bed between my legs so he can bend down closer. He encircles one breast with his hand, and even with how big his palms are, my flesh bulges out between his fingers.

I've always hated them, my big boobs. It's hard to find bras that fit my tiny ribcage, and everyone stares at them. But right now, I don't want anything else but Banon's hungry gaze on me as he rolls my nipple between two of his fingers.

"These are incredible." Gently, he pushes me down onto the bed and crawls on top of me, spreading his hooves out to either side of my legs. His tail flicks back and forth behind him eagerly. "I've always wanted to suck on them."

"Then do it," I whisper, and he does. He puts

his whole big mouth around one breast, drawing the nipple between his lips and sucking. I gasp as he palms my other breast, plucking it, teasing it, drawing out this tiny spark of pleasure bigger and bigger as he switches sides, rolling my other nipple around with his tongue before gently nibbling on it. Soon my hands are buried in his mane as he plays and torments me.

"I want you to take all your clothes off," he says, reaching between us to tug at my pants. "I want to lick every part of you."

The suggestion of what he might do between my legs sends a ripple of excitement through me. I never could have imagined Banon, that big muscle head, eating me out.

He stands up so I can do as I'm told, wriggling off my pajama pants and dropping them onto the floor. I reach for my socks, too, but he holds onto my ankle and stops me.

"No, I like the socks." He drags his palms up my legs, to my thighs, where my underwear still clings to me. "You missed a spot."

He hooks his fingers in the band, then lifts my legs so he can slowly drag them down. As he goes, he peppers my thighs with kisses, until the panties are off my feet and he shucks them across the room.

"You're still dressed." I nod at his shirt and jeans. "Don't I get to look, too?"

He grins that arrogant grin that I've always loved, and eagerly pulls his shirt off over his head, the neck wide enough to slip over his horns. His jeans go next, falling down his haunches to his hooves.

His briefs don't hide much, but it's still too much covering him up.

"You want more?" he asks, bending down to tilt my chin up, so I'm looking into his eyes. "Do you want to see my cock again, Valentina?"

I'll never get used to the way he says that name.

I nod, because I do. I want to get to touch it, and do many, many other things with it.

Still smirking, Banon pulls his boxer briefs down, and that massive cock emerges, hanging down but curving away from his body. I know it only gets bigger from here.

For a moment, I wonder how he's going to fit. He's much larger than any of the other males I've slept with since I went away to college, even that sphinx guy who lives on the bottom floor.

Watching me curiously, Banon reaches down and strokes himself, fingers traveling from the thick base to the blunt tip, where a bead of white fluid gathers at the slit. I sit forward on the bed so I can reach, then gently settle my hands on it. He sits back, letting me have his cock all to myself.

"It's huge," I whisper, running a palm from the root to the head.

"Don't worry." Banon strokes my cheek, over my ear and down to my jaw. "I'll get you ready for it."

That tingle in my abdomen is spreading, and I know right then that I want this inside me. I need Banon more than I need anything, or I might just starve.

Encircling him with my fingers, I admire his fat cock, how veins spider up the sides, underneath which hang two huge, furry balls. While I stroke with one hand, I reach down and cup them in my palm, testing their weight.

"Damn," Banon grunts. "You know just how to touch me."

I squeeze harder, moving faster while I massage him. He bites his hand to quiet a groan, and even more of his pre-cum beads at the tip. Now it's dripping down the underside, giving my hand plenty of lube.

"Shit," he says suddenly, grabbing my wrist to

still my movements. "I'm going to come all over you if you keep doing that."

I quirk an eyebrow. "You don't want to?"

"Not like this." He takes both my hands in his, our fingers interlocking. "When I come, I want it to be inside you."

Oh, I see. I want that, too, so I let him push me back down onto the bed. I think that he's finally going to give me what I've been craving, what I've been thirsting for all these years, but then he picks me up by the ass with one hand and grabs my thigh in the other, pushing my legs apart. I'm completely bare to him, and who knows how long it's been since I shaved? I decided in college that I wasn't going to wax and shave my naturally occurring hair, but now I regret it. Cheerleaders are always waxed to perfection, I'm sure.

Banon's face lights up, and his tongue skims across his lower lip. "Au naturale," he says, his hand trailing up the inside of my thigh. "Very good."

Good? That's not what I expected him to say.

He finally reaches the apex of my thighs, and there, he spreads my labia with two fingers. He studies me, and I'm tempted to snap my legs closed again at the intent look on his face, when he bends forward and dives in.

Immediately, his tongue whirls over my clit, and it's thick and broad and shockingly dexterous. It's just a ghost of a touch, though, the beginning of one.

"Banon," I whimper.

He groans against me. "I've always wanted to hear you say my name like that." He spreads me even farther apart as he licks me again, harder, back and forth and up and down and around and around, until I'm gasping and my body is twitching on its own.

"Mmm." Banon lifts his head, his big muzzle dripping. "Damn. I've thought about tasting that forever." The hand that's been spreading me drops lower, the pad of his finger coasting over that empty place inside me. He nudges at my entrance. "You're already so wet."

I'm too drunk on sex at present to tell him that he's always done this to me, that I get my panties damp just sitting in the same car. But the sight of his horns poking up between my thighs, his shaggy hair moving as he goes down on me, is definitely lubing me up.

He applies more pressure with his finger, and I'm surprised by just how thick it is as he pushes it through my outer folds, asking me to open until he's sunk in me up to his knuckle. I gasp around it, and Banon grins before he returns to his work.

Now his finger and tongue are dancing in tandem, winding me up tighter and making every wet thrust louder and louder. Just that one finger and the expert teasing of that tongue is sending me rocketing, a live wire, writhing and whimpering.

"Going to come for me?" he says over my mound. He pumps his finger harder, then curls it at the tip, dragging it along my upper wall as he plays me like a fiddle.

"Yes, yes." I bite down on my lip to keep from making too much sound, even though Dad and Marissa's bedroom is down the other hall.

To my vast indignation, Banon slows down. That's when I feel a second finger asking for entry. I'm so wet, though, that it has no problem sliding in, filling me up even further.

"There," he murmurs. "Let's get you ready."

Once more, Banon attacks me, flicking his tongue faster and harder as his two fingers work together. Now they're both curling, both stimulating that wonderful place deep down inside me. Only one girl has ever done this, but she did not have sausage-sized fingers. He's so thick that I'm teetering, sliding closer to the edge, gripping the blankets as Banon ravages me.

How does he know how to do this? Just thinking about it makes me jealous—wondering how many other women he's pleasured this way, brought to the breaking point this way.

"Fuck," Banon growls, lifting his head again. "Nobody tastes like you, Valentina. Nobody in the whole goddamned world." God, he has such a wonderfully dirty mouth.

He buries his fingers inside me, truly fucking me with them as he eats me up. Every single thought is gone, poof, vanished from my brain as his hand slicks in and out, his tongue going wild, and I smoosh my lips together to not cry out when it hits me like a train.

"Mmmph!" I manage, covering my mouth with one hand. Between my legs, Banon moans, his fingers pumping even faster.

"That's right, give it all to me." He slurps me up, and I should be horrified at the sound, but it's drawing out my incredible orgasm even further.

Finally, he lowers me back to the bed, and I go utterly boneless.

"I haven't come like that ever," I whisper to

the ceiling as Banon plops himself down next to me. He is still, surprisingly, rock-hard.

"Damn," I say, rolling over onto my side so we're face to face. I reach down and wrap my hand around his dick, just marveling at its size.

"Your little moans got me going." He grips my ass and pulls my naked hips against his, his cock pressed to my belly, my hand trapped between us. "Now I just want to fuck you. Make you moan even more."

I know we need to keep our voices down, but all his dirty talk is turning me on.

"But I can't make noise!" I whisper.

His lip quirks on one side. "I'll make sure you don't wake anybody up."

Banon kisses me then, grinding his slick cock against me as he dominates my mouth. Soon, I'm on my back and he's rolled on top of me, both of us panting.

"Now, Valentina," he murmurs, sliding down so his hips are planted between my thighs, "it might not fit at first. But I'll make sure it does."

CHAPTER
SEVEN

BANON

Valentina. I say her name again and again in my head as I gaze down at her, spread out before me with her big, brown nipples, and a pop of curly hair between her legs. Her belly moves with each of her heavy breaths. Those bottomless eyes are watching me, lids hooded so I can make out each of her long lashes.

I almost want to lick her again, taste her again, drink her up and make her come over and over. But that's for later. That's for next time. For the next one million times.

No, I need to be inside her, now.

Suddenly, she turns and reaches for the bedside table. "A condom, right?" That's what she thinks I was hesitating over. "I'm sure teenage me had some in here."

I reach out and grab her outstretched hand, wrapping mine around it and drawing her back to me.

"Banon?" she asks, perplexed.

"I've always worn a condom. Always." I bite out this last word, so she knows I have never faltered in my duty. "Every woman I've ever slept with. But not with you, Valentina. I want yours to be the first pussy I feel—really feel. I've been saving it for you."

Val inhales sharply, and she searches my face for what might be behind my words. I can still sense her skepticism.

"Well, it's not like you can get me pregnant," she says, slowly relaxing. "You promise you've been tested?"

I growl low in my throat at the idea that I've ever let myself be exposed that way. Lowering my head, I rumble into her ear, "I haven't fucked a woman in a year, Valentina. Too obsessed with you. Too busy thinking about you."

She gasps. "Me?"

"Yeah, you. I get tested, but I don't need it to

tell me what I already know." I lean forward so my cock sits right between her legs. "That I can't make myself fuck anyone but you."

And I can't wait any longer.

Val squeaks when I grab her thighs and spread them wide, creating enough room for my hips. God damn. I can't believe I finally get to have the woman of my dreams. That I get to see her like this, each gorgeous inch of her bare, golden skin, and I get to show her with every fiber of my being how goddamned much I love her.

"Now remember," I tell her as I rub the head of my cock over her clit, making her squirm. "Keep quiet. Bite me if you have to."

"Bite you?" she whispers.

"Whatever you need to do." The very last thing I want is for my mother to walk in on this. "Now, sweet Valentina, I am going to finally do what I've been dreaming of doing for much, much longer than I'm willing to admit to you."

She smiles at this. "Then do it, Banon."

I tease her to rile her up again, wetting my cock in her and then skating it up and down, over her clit and back again, until she's whining and her hips are trying to bring me inside her.

Finally, I settle right there, spreading apart the lips of her pussy, and carefully push in.

Immediately, there's resistance, because she is tiny and I am not tiny. But, as terrible as I feel admitting it, I have had sex with human women many times before. I know it works if I give it time.

"Oh shit," Val says, gripping my arm. "I don't know if you'll fit."

I place a single, gentle kiss on her lips. "I will." I stay at the shallowest depth possible, so I'm barely sheathed inside her, and simply rock back and forth. Her mouth forms an O as I fully withdraw, then push in again. If I can loosen her up one centimeter at a time...

"Ohh," she moans as I press in just a tiny bit deeper. When I pull out, I tease her clit before sliding inside her once more. I'm going to take my time pleasing this woman. I'm going to open her up for me until all she wants is my cock buried in her up to the hilt.

Her head thrashes on the bed, haloed by her dark hair. "Banon!" she whisper-cries. Her legs hook over my hips as she tries to bring me in deeper.

"Shh," I whisper to her. "We have to teach

you to take me. Then I'm going to stretch this pussy out so nobody else can fill it but me."

Valentina gasps as my words make her clench around me. I can feel every last inch of her, how just the warmth that encompasses my head is textured inside in the most delicious way. I squeeze more of myself through, and those swollen, pink lips spread even wider for me. Valentina moans, clearly trying to muffle herself by squeezing her lips together, but still the sound comes out.

I reel back, and already I'm leaking rather gratuitously. She does this to me, makes me want to let off too soon, when normally I am the king of self-control. I rub my cum all over her before sliding in once again, asking more of her soft body to allow me through.

"Oh god." She covers her mouth with her hand. Her hips buck as I explore further, soaking up the pulse of her, the throbbing vigor for life inside her that can't help bubbling up to the surface wherever she goes. This time, when I thrust in, I push through almost halfway, and her back arches.

It's a scene I never could have summoned, even in my dreams. I pause there, only partway encased in her, and palm her perfect breasts.

They're so much better than I imagined, and I simply worship them as I let her body get accustomed to me.

"Please, Banon." Val grasps my arms tight. "Please!"

"Whatever she asks," I whisper, pulling my hips back, then thrusting into her, gliding in as deep as I can. I cover her mouth with mine just in time to swallow her cry, and I can't fucking believe how good she feels, how absolutely mind-bogglingly perfect it is to be inside her. She's hot and wet and wonderfully *her*, and I kiss her harder as I slowly, methodically, pull out and then sink in, withdraw and push through, and every single time, she gives to me, parting for me, squeezing all around me with the rhythm of her racing pulse.

If I were to die at any moment, at least I've done this, and shown her how my heart only beats because she's here.

VALENTINA

Truly, I can't believe this is my life. Banon's on top of me, my legs spread around his incredible, huge body, his ripped abdomen flexing with every careful pump of his hips. His eyes are laser-focused on me as he sits back on his knees, cupping my breasts, enveloping my hips, squeezing my ass. Each time he delves inside me with that fat cock, I have to hold back my cries, because I've never felt so beautifully *full*. It's as if something I've been seeking all my life has finally found me and now I want more, and more, until there's nothing left but me and him in the entire world.

Banon's right—I'll never have sex with someone like this again, not as long as I live.

He kisses me again as he picks up his pace, curling his arms underneath me so our chests are flush together. He dwarfs me, the muscles of his tree-trunk arms tensing with every movement, the tips of his horns occasionally tapping the headboard. Somehow, there's even more of him, and even more again as he fits that massive thing inside me, pushing it in farther with every powerful shunt of his hips.

"You're so perfect," he mutters, bringing my head in closer to his neck like he can't bear to be even a few inches apart. "Everything I've ever wanted. Everything I've ever needed."

Then he's all the way there, so deep that I

can't possibly make any more room for him, and I do it—I bite into his shoulder, trying to keep the building scream in my throat at bay.

My minotaur chuckles, nudging me with his muzzle. "That's right, Valentina. Let go for me. I'll carry you there."

"Banon," I whimper. "I've never felt anything like it, like *you*—" I'm cut off as he picks up his pace, rooting me to the bed with one hand under my neck and the other gripping my hip.

"I know, baby." Somehow, he holds me even closer. Nobody's ever fucked me like this, like I'm the most precious thing in the universe. "Me neither. You were made for me."

I think that he's right when his furry balls slap my ass, which means he's buried in me as far as he can be. I've taken all of it, every last inch of him, and it feels so fantastic that I might implode. He stretches every edge as he thrusts in, both of us so wet that I can hear it as he bottoms out. At this angle, with my thighs spread and his hips pounding into me, he's rubbing over that same spot inside me that his fingers did, and it's shooting off shockwaves to every last corner of my body. I keep my teeth locked in his flesh as I hold back another shout, because I'm so overwhelmed with the bliss of being together that I can barely control what's coming out of my mouth.

"That's right. Keep quiet and choke my cock." He grunts each time he shoves himself in, his own moans growing as I get closer and closer, my body tightening and straining as he mercilessly, relentlessly takes me. Owns me. Fucks me into oblivion.

Damn. I think I love him, too. I hope this isn't a one-time event, a singular moment in time that we won't get to have again, because it will be utterly impossible to let him go after this.

My overwhelming affection for this big minotaur on top of me nearly bowls me over, and there are tears in my eyes as my orgasm crawls closer and closer, waiting to leap and envelop me. I cling to him tighter, hoping that I can hold on to him like this forever.

"Please, please," I whine against his throat, my arms wrapped tight around his neck. I don't know what I'm asking for, but maybe it's a prayer that this moment never ends. "Banon, I —" Bliss is racing up my spine, spreading into my fingers and toes, and a wire inside me is stretched as far as it can be. "I think I—"

"It's okay, baby," he answers, never slowing,

never relenting in his glorious rhythm. "I won't run away."

I choke as a tear spills down my cheek. "I love you," I say, my voice hoarse. "So much."

I can feel Banon smile against me. He ratchets up his speed, now fucking me so hard and so fast that the bed is creaking.

"I love you too, Valentina."

Just those words do me in. The wire snaps, and a torrent sweeps down on me, sucking me under. Banon moans atop me, plunging in with all the power stored up in his big body, as I clench tighter and tighter.

"Yes, baby, yes. Come around me. Gush on me."

I can't help obeying as my climax consumes me. I try my hardest not to scream, biting my own tongue to keep it in as Banon fucks me through it.

"Oh fuck, oh fuck," he rasps. "I'm going to stuff you full. Going to give you everything."

"Yes, yes!" I try to keep my voice down, but I can't feel anything under my skin except for glorious pleasure, and I want whatever he has to offer me.

Banon's fingers curl into claws, digging into my flesh as he bites down on the pillow. He thrusts hard, sinking in until his fur is brushing my clit, and groans as his cock swells even thicker inside me. I squeal as it triggers another miniature orgasm, bliss radiating out from the place we're connected. Banon holds me even tighter against him, like I might get ripped away, as he plows into me one last time.

"Valentina," he moans, twitching and spasming as he finishes. I feel cum trickle out, down my ass to the comforter underneath me. One of his arms gives out, and he rests some of his immense weight on me, which nearly knocks the breath from my lungs.

"Banon!" I gasp for air. "I can't... breathe..."

"Shit." He hurriedly picks himself up, his immense cock still heavy inside me. "Sorry. Don't know my own size."

He moves to withdraw, but I grab him to stop him. I don't want him to leave me, not yet. Not when I worry that I'll wake up and find this was all a dream.

Banon blinks down at me, then a smile turns up his lips.

"You like the feeling of me filling up your sweet little pussy?" he asks, leaning down to peck my cheek.

All I can do is nod, because nothing has ever

felt so right. We remain like that as he slowly deflates, then eventually slides out.

Banon rolls onto his side, bringing me with him. I stroke the fur of his chest, his bicep soft and pillow-like under my head.

"I'll have to go soon," he whispers, kissing the top of my head.

"Yeah, I know." I sigh, both content and resigned.

"Don't worry." He skims one hand down my side, to my hip and then up again in a soothing gesture. "I can come pick you up from school anytime. Rich is gone most nights at his girl-friend's place."

I perk up at the suggestion that we can do this again—and maybe even somewhere I don't have to stay quiet.

"You mean it?" I ask.

"Of course I mean it. I want to do this with you forever." He pulls me even closer, like I'm a teddy bear he wants to keep close. "Now that I've had you, I'm never letting you go."

Movement of any kind is impossible as Banon climbs out of my bed and picks his jeans up off the floor. I watch with displeasure as he dresses again, because I wish more than anything that he could sleep beside me.

"I'm sorry," he says at the sight of my morose expression. He crouches by the bed and kisses me on the lips, then the nose, then the forehead. "Next time, I'll be right next to you."

Then he opens the door, slipping out so he can return to his own room.

I lie awake for some time after he's gone, wondering if this was real. What if it was just tonight? What if what happened here disappears in the light of day?

If it doesn't—if I really heard Banon right when he said he loved me, too—my life has just gotten a lot more complicated. What would Dad do if he found out about this? What if next time Marissa hears us and walks in?

I shove my face into the pillow, trying to remember only the good things. I can worry about the rest later.

CHAPTER
EIGHT

BANON

'm in a daze as I open the door to our shared bathroom and then shut it quietly behind me before entering my own room. My walls are darker than Val's, a slate gray, with dark curtains. Sports posters pepper my walls—football players I admired once upon a time, but who now seem so... mortal.

I fall back onto my bed, my dick perfectly happy and satisfied, just like my heart is. Damn. I didn't think sex could *be* like that. I didn't think it could expose you so deeply, bring you so close to someone else that you feel like you can see inside them.

Tonight, I saw Valentina. I peered in through a window to her soul and she saw right into mine, and we danced our dance together in the way that rock songs talk about.

But it isn't long of looking up at my ceiling before the darkness of the world outside pours in. What we did just now... it was the best thing to ever happen to me. And yet no one can find out. Nobody can know what Val and I have done together, the kinds of feelings we harbor toward each other.

I should fall asleep right away after a doozy like that, but those thoughts keep me up for hours. What would I say if Mom and Fred found out? Fuck. She's his twenty-one-year-old daughter. He would certainly have some thoughts about that.

Falling asleep doesn't register at all in my memory. What does is waking up to sun coming in my window, extra bright because it's reflecting off the snow that fell last night.

My eyes feel heavy and laden from not sleeping. I drag myself out of bed, hoping for some coffee at least. Mom is already in the kitchen busying about, getting ready to make her famous pancakes.

"Oh, you look like you need this," she says,

grabbing a mug before I've even sat down at the table. She fills it up from the pot and deposits it in front of me, rubbing my back before returning to her work. I've never been much of a morning minotaur, and I love Mom even more for remembering that.

Then Fred comes in, as chipper as ever, and calls out, "Good morning, Banon!" He's cheery now, but wait until he finds out I'm banging his daughter.

Goddamn it. It was so good, so *fucking* good, so absolutely right to be with her—and it might have been the biggest mistake of my life. I can't even look Fred in the eye as he pulls out the eggs and starts cooking, not after what I did with Val last night.

I shouldn't have done it. I should never have opened that door between us. I have to figure out how to shut it, for both of our safety, for the safety of this family.

VALENTINA

The next morning, I practically leap out of bed, completely rested and ready for the day. Sex with

Banon last night was like the best drug possible. I slept like the dead, and right now, the world is my oyster. I am a new woman with a new lease on life.

I come out of my room bright-eyed and bushy-tailed. I smell eggs cooking, and I hope it comes with pancakes. Marissa makes the best banana nut pancakes.

As I come down the hall, I can hear my dad laughing as Marissa says, "And then Robert told him to find his own plumber!"

I'm clearly the last one to arrive. As I'd hoped, my stepmother is in front of the stove-top, flipping a pancake, a stack of cooked ones beside her. Dad is taking off the eggs and spooning them out onto plates. They both look cheery—but then I notice Banon at the table.

He's leaned over his coffee, dark circles under his eyes. He glances up when I arrive, and his brows rise, his mouth twitching up in a smile. But then, as he looks around the kitchen where Dad and Marissa are busying about, it falls from his face and he stares down at the placemat.

The pep drops out of my step. I hope he doesn't regret last night. Oh, god, I hope everything is all right after how we left it. It seemed like he was excited for the future, but now he looks like the Cryptkeeper.

"Good morning," I say, forcing myself to sound chipper. I smile at Banon, hoping he'll return it, but he simply drinks his orange juice.

"Morning, sunshine," Dad says. "OJ?"

He pours me a glass of orange juice, and I join Banon at the table. We put the leaf away so I can sit close and not look too awkward. Under the table, I put a hand on Banon's knee.

The minotaur tenses all over, his eyes darting to mine. He tips his head and then shakes it. A clear message: *don't do that*.

My hand drops to my side. What's going on? What happened?

So it *was* just a dream. Just a stupid fucking dream.

I try not to let it show on my face how miserable that feels, smiling and nodding when Dad and Marissa serve up the food. They talk to me and I do my best to process it, answering accordingly while the entire back of my brain wonders, *Why? Why would he do that with me?*

Maybe I was right. Maybe it was the ultimate humiliation, a joke he was playing on me, after all.

"Banon, will you take Val back to school on

your way home?" Dad asks as I plate up bacon and pancakes, slathering them with maple syrup.

"Sure," he says, then yawns. "No problem."

I try to catch his eye, but Banon carefully looks away from me, and I become more certain that everything that happened in my childhood bedroom was a huge mistake. But I maintain the façade as we finish breakfast, then head to my room to pack up. Banon's waiting by the front door and doesn't speak as we head out to his car.

I don't even know what to say when we shut the doors and he peels away from the curb. I'm too shocked, too hurt, to even open my mouth. I think over everything I might say as he speeds toward my school, but it all sounds pathetic.

I'm so pathetic, thinking he would love me in the light of day.

The entire ride is silent, all the way until Banon pulls up outside my dorm. I sit there in the passenger seat, unmoving, trying not to break down.

"Really?" I finally ask. "Like we don't even know each other?"

"Val..." Banon grips the steering wheel tighter. "We can't do this. I stayed up all night thinking about it, and I decided. We can't."

I knew it. I knew it was all too good, too right, and I couldn't have that. Not with him.

"Cool." I don't know what else to say. "You decided on your own. So you're gonna use me and toss me, like every girl you've ever fucked. Got it."

His head swivels toward me. "It's not like that."

"Then how is it?" I am trying my damnedest not to cry, because he doesn't deserve my tears. "Please, explain it to me. How *you* came to my room. How *you* told me beautiful lies, and now you regret it. Tell me all about it."

He sets his broad teeth together and hisses between them. "We'll be ostracized! Everyone will judge us. It will be a war all our lives just to be recognized. And that doesn't even count my mom and your dad—what would *they* say? Wouldn't they be... disgusted with us?"

He's panting after laying it all out on the table. Of course, I know that he's right. I didn't want to think about it too hard, but it would be an uphill battle for us. Still, I wanted to try. I wanted to fight for this, because I thought I could believe in it.

But he doesn't.

"I'm sorry," he says, bowing his head. "I'm

sorry I came to your room. I should never have said what I said on the park bench."

It hurts even more, knowing that he regrets it.

"Valentina." Banon turns fully in his seat, checking out the window over my shoulder before he leans down toward me. "I didn't lie about anything. I love you. But I can't have you."

I don't need to put up with this.

"If you loved me, you would try for me," I say, getting my wits about me again. "I don't care whether the world knows or not."

I pull away from him, grabbing my backpack out of the footwell. I'm over this.

"You'd keep it a secret?" he asks as I grab the door handle. "You'd want that?"

I could just shake him.

"I want *you*." I glare over my shoulder. "That's it, Banon. That's all I've ever wanted. I would rather have that than pretending nothing ever happened, and spending my whole life wondering what could have been."

He's quiet, simply watching me, his eyes searching mine for something. I know he knows it—the way we fit together, how it was life-altering in a way that can never be undone. What we did was irreversible, and we'll both be haunted by it forever.

The sternness on Banon's face falters, and he buckles forward.

"Whatever I have to do," he says, sounding choked. "If I get to keep you, I'll do it. If it means I never tell another soul about you, I'll do it." He reaches out and grabs my hand, squeezing it like it's his very last lifeline. "I'm sorry, Val. All I want is to keep you safe. I don't want you to destroy your reputation for me." He squints. "I already did that once."

"Then no one will find out." I peek out the window, too, to make sure we're alone before putting my hands on his big muzzle and pulling him in for a kiss. It's quick, so we don't get caught, but exactly what I needed.

Putting on my backpack, I open the car door and step out.

"Next time Rich is gone at his girlfriend's place," Banon says in a low voice, "do you want to come over?"

"Just text me." I hold up my phone. "I'll be ready."

I'm in my Calculus II class the next Monday when my phone buzzes in my pocket.

> Rich is going on a date and won't be back. Could I pick you up?

I glance at the prof before answering.

> I'll be ready at six.

> Great. I'll grab dinner on the way.

I'm buzzing throughout the rest of my classes, eager to get back to my room and change. I have the perfect bra and panty set, much cuter than what I was wearing the other night, though I doubt I'll be wearing them for long.

Finally, I'm done. I take a quick shower and even blow-dry my hair, which requires borrowing a blow-dryer because I've never bothered to use one before. Then I slip on a cute dress with long sleeves and a pair of matching leggings with knee-high boots.

When Banon's car stops at the curb, he rolls down the window and mimes removing a pair of sunglasses.

"Fire alarm's about to go off," he says as I open the door and hop in.

I glance around. "How do you know that? Did you see some smoke?"

A laugh bursts out of him, and Banon nearly falls forward against the steering wheel as he continues snorting like a bull. "No, I just meant you look hot."

"Oh." I feel like a dumbass. "What food did you get?"

"Thai. Your favorite, the massaman curry."

"Perfect." He does know me well.

When we get to the apartment, I manage to keep my hands to myself until we're inside. Banon sets the food on the half wall in the entryway while I take off my boots, then he sweeps me into his arms and pins me against the door.

"Damn," he mutters, one hand dragging over my tits, squeezing them and releasing them. "I want to rip your clothes off right fucking now."

I grip the collar of his shirt. "Then do it."

With a growl, Banon slips one hand under my dress and hikes it up, then pushes down my leggings with the other. He investigates my underwear between my legs, rubbing me through them. I twitch and gasp, and his mouth curves up in a smirk.

"This time, I get to hear you scream." He pulls my panties down next, so both end up on the floor. He unbuttons his jeans, sliding them down his ass just enough that his cock jumps free and his tail flicks wildly behind him. That thick bull cock of his swells and rises between us. Then he grabs me by the ass and lifts me into the air, slamming my back against the door.

"Are you ready for me, Valentina?" he asks, lining himself up without even using his hands. "Do you think your pussy can take me?"

"I know I can." I reach down to position his cock right where it needs to be, and with a grunt, Banon slides home.

CHAPTER
NINE

BANON

Her pussy is so good, I could simply drown in it. But we've only fucked once before, so I try to keep my enthusiasm at a reasonable level as I slide inside her.

Valentina's moan is the most beautiful music. I test to make sure she's wet enough before I push deeper, and she swallows me like a soft glove. Her legs wrap around my hips, which has the delicious effect of bringing me in even farther.

Our few days apart were miserable. My body was primed to mate after fucking her the first time, sinking into her without a condom and then covering her in my cum. Now, the need is nearly overwhelming. I'll have to focus hard not to finish too soon.

I hold Valentina pinned as I wade deeper, then pull out, then deeper again to get her lubed. I'll fuck her with my tongue later, but right now, I need to paint her with my smell again.

She moans as I wedge myself in deep, then pick up my pace, her ass bumping the door with every thrust. Now she doesn't have to hold back and Valentina rewards me, crying out when I'm sunk in her up to the base.

She's so good, so blissfully tight and throbbing with her breaths, that I'm struggling to hold out. Usually, I have excellent stamina, but as her voice climbs higher and she comes closer to her orgasm, clenching so obscenely around me, I can't do it anymore.

"Val, I'm sorry," I manage to say, right before I unload. Everything comes streaming out of me in a torrent, and I grunt and slam into her again, getting my cum as deep in her as possible. I know I can't knock her up—humans and minotaurs and everything—but damn, my animal brain loves the idea.

"Shit." I lean back, gathering Val up in my

arms, still inside her. "That was not what I expected to happen."

She giggles, then moans when my cock twitches. "It's okay."

"No, it is not." I carry her into the living room and lower her back to the couch, my cock slipping out of her. My cum gets all over the cushions, but I'll deal with that later. I pull up her dress, and her pussy is wonderfully pink, all swollen and dripping with me. I lean down and drag my tongue over her clit.

Val's back bows. I do it again, this time sliding three fingers inside her. I really stretched her good and open for me. She clenches as I lick her harder, and she gasps out my name.

Just the sound of it makes my mane stand up.

Each thrust of my fingers makes a wet noise, as filled as she is with my cum. Her pussy clamps down around my hand as my tongue speeds up, and she grabs onto my horns with both hands.

"Banon, yes, please, yes," she chants like a prayer. Her thighs tighten around my head as she gets closer and closer, and then, she cries out. It's like the most beautiful song, her voice letting the world know that I've pleased her, and her tiny pussy squeezes down around me with impressive power.

I can't wait for her to wrap around my cock like that again. I'll have to jack off more when she's not around, build up my tolerance in wake of how unbelievably perfect she feels.

I wipe my lips and sit up, gazing down at where Valentina lies with the dress of her skirt pulled up around her hips, her pussy glistening with our fluids. Damn, she's beautiful like that. I mean, she's always beautiful, but she's especially beautiful with her face blissed-out, her thighs askew, wanton and leaking with me.

I'm absolutely feral for this woman.

Getting a towel from the kitchen, I wet it in the sink and bring it over. Val's eyes flutter open, and she smiles softly as I clean her.

"I forgot about the food," she says with a grin.

"Believe me, I didn't." I toss the towel away and kiss her on the lips. "I just had more important matters to attend to first."

After eating dinner, we lie on the couch together to watch a movie. But it isn't long before my hands are wandering, playing absently with Val's big tits, cradling her hip, testing her between the legs to see if she's warm and wet yet.

"Hey," she whispers. "Do you want to watch the movie or not?"

"I guess not." I tug her onto her back and then roll on top of her, so she's trapped between me and the soft couch cushions. "Actually, yeah, definitely not."

We manage to make it to my bed after another round on the couch. God, I can't get enough of her. I want to live with my cock buried inside her, soaking her up while she moans and cries out my name.

On the bed, I take her from behind, admiring her pussy spread wide around me, her tiny asshole pulsing. Maybe she'll let me use a butt plug on her. I know she'd like it.

When I fall asleep that night, it's covered in sweat with my arm curled around my sweet woman, my confident, gorgeous, absolutely brilliant woman, and I'm glad that I can have this, for now.

The next morning, though, she has to get going early, before Rich potentially comes home to shower and change for work. That means my alarm goes off right at six, and a groggy, grumpy Valentina puts on her clothes and stumbles out the front door with me before we can run into my roommate. Then I drive her back to school, all before getting home and then pretending to climb back into bed.

I hope we never accidentally oversleep. I've known Rich since my freshman year of college, and he's watched Valentina grow up into the woman she is now. He would definitely judge me if he caught her sneaking out of the apartment, hair all mussed like she got fucked into the mattress many times over.

But we get away with it. Thank god we get away with it.

The first hiccup in the road comes when Val wants to come see me play. She's never attended one of my football games before, and I wonder what the other guys will think when she starts showing up.

"I want to watch you," she says, eyelashes fluttering. "Come on. I saw you play in high school. I know how great you look doing it."

Val sure knows how to give a male an ego.

"Fine." I have no choice but to relent. There's nothing wrong with it—but it means my worlds will cross, for better or worse.

It's the last big game before Christmas break, and by the time the sun goes down, the air is full of a light mist. Wet playing fields are never a good thing.

As we file out onto the astroturf, I check the stands for signs of Val. She's near the front, a pretty decent seat, and she waves shyly as I pass. I incline my chin in her direction, but I need to get my head in the game.

Despite the rain, I play good and I play hard, throwing killer tosses, catching balls I have no right reaching. I even get a solid sprint in, clearing half the football field before I'm stopped by a pile-on.

My brains are a little rattled by that, but it's nothing special. I feel like a brand new minotaur, completely rewritten by this woman who I can finally call mine.

She's waiting for me by the door to the locker rooms, bouncing on the balls of her feet after our big win tonight.

"Go wait outside," I tell her. The rest of the team is going to jump on her like coyotes on a fresh kill. She's smoking hot and technically not taken. Ripe for the picking.

The smile on her face wavers, and she looks confused. "Outside...?"

"Who's that?" one of the other players calls

out, an orc fellow who's usually nice enough, but he talks just as much shit about fooling around with the cheerleaders as anybody else in the locker room. Which means I don't want him near Val.

"Seeing a new girl, Banon?" the orc asks.

I huff, wishing we could have avoided this. "My stepsister. Val."

He brightens up like I've just given him a gift. "Oh, your stepsister?" He comes up to us, hand extended in Val's direction. "Nice to meet you. I'm Louie."

She politely shakes his hand, throwing me an apologetic look.

"What are you two doing after this?" he asks.

"Um, getting some dinner." Val looks wildly uncomfortable now, which is how I feel, too. Just watching Louie talking to her with that hungry wolf look on his face makes me want to punch him in the head.

"Oh, maybe I could tag along?" He arches an eyebrow. "I'd love to get to know you a bit, Val."

He couldn't be more shameless if he tried.

"Louie," I say in a low, threatening tone. "It's family business. Go get showered."

He furrows his brow, glancing between us before he shrugs, like none of this matters anyway. "All right. See ya at practice, Banon." He salutes before taking off into the locker room.

I let out a sigh of relief. Val pats me on the shoulder before she scurries off, clearly eager not to attract any more attention.

But that doesn't stop the guys from teasing me when I get to the locker room.

"Your sister's hot for being human," Louie says as I step under the hot water.

"She's not my sister. She's my *step*sister. Notice that I am not human?"

"Yeah, yeah. Still, you should give me her number."

I want to roar my fury and tell him not to get anywhere near Val, that if he even so much as touches her, he's a dead fucking orc—but that would be ridiculous.

"I'll pass," I say instead.

"Her loss," says Louie as he turns off his shower head and steps out. I grunt at his retreating back, glad he's gone so I don't have to keep fantasizing about ripping his head off his shoulders.

After a quick shower, I throw my clothes back on and high-five a few of my teammates on the way out for our killer win tonight.

"You rocked, Banon."

"The star college quarterback strikes again."

"Thanks, guys." I wave goodbye as I step out into the cool night.

There, instead of finding Val waiting for me, a few of the girls from the cheerleading squad are hanging out off to one side, showing each other videos on their phones.

"Oh, Banon!" Megan hops off the wall where she's been perched in her tiny skirt and even tinier top. "I was wondering when you were gonna show up. I didn't hear from you that night before Thanksgiving."

Right. I completely forgot that Megan had given me her number. She was the one I was talking about when I mentioned a cheerleader with a great ass, but in absolutely no way does her ass compare to Val's.

Fuck. I get hard just thinking about it. How soft it is under my hands, how it bulges out when I squeeze it while I'm inside her...

"Yeah, sorry, got busy with things." It's the most noncommittal answer I can give without being rude and outright telling her I'm not interested. I'd been a little curious before, because she does have a good rack and nice butt, but nothing could be less tempting now. I just want to get out of here and meet up with Val by the car.

"Well," Megan says, sauntering over to me, "it's not too late." She pokes my chest with her index finger, drawing it up to my collarbone and throat, then to my chin.

I don't like how casually she's touching me. The hair on my mane stands on end, and I resist the urge to slap her hand away.

Val's voice interrupts us. "You ready yet?" She approaches from the parking lot, pausing when she sees the three cheerleaders still in their uniforms. Megan is standing obnoxiously close, and I don't like how this situation must look, not at all.

"Who's this?" asks Megan, her brows lowering as she regards Val. I know mean-girl behavior when I see it, and the train is already in motion.

"My stepsister, Valentina." I back away, heading over to where Val is waiting by the curb. "We're, uh, going out to dinner to celebrate my win."

"Oh, that's fun!" Her expression totally changes now that she doesn't think Val is a threat. "Maybe I could come along?"

This is the second person trying to get in the

way of our nice dinner, and I'm starting to get pissed.

"No." I say it flatly, without room for argument, and Megan's mouth bobs open. "Bye. See you at the next game."

Then I turn and head off toward the car, wishing I could grab Val's hand and pull her along with me.

CHAPTER
TEN

VALENTINA

I knew right away when I saw that cheerleader invading my boyfriend's personal space that she's the one with the nice ass. Banon must have been cruising to hook up with her before Thanksgiving.

A part of me deflates, seeing her up close. She's really fucking hot. Insanely hot. Her hair was up in a ponytail but still a million times more put-together than mine, with flouncy little curls. She had a long, shapely neck, normal-sized tits, and a body with absolutely perfect proportions, like a cover model.

She's definitely Banon's type, with dark

brown hair and brown eyes, golden-brown skin and...

I blink as we walk to the car. Hmm. I guess that could also describe *me*, if I were taller and had skinnier thighs.

"Don't think anything about it," Banon says, breaking the silence as we approach his car in the lot. "I can see the gears turning in your head."

"Think what about what?" I ask innocently.

"About Megan. I never hooked up with her."

I raise both my hands. "I didn't say you did."

"I know. But I just want to be clear. I really haven't been with anyone but you since last year."

It's sweet that he's trying to reassure me, and my ego does appreciate it after seeing what that girl had on display.

The moment we're both in the car, Banon shuts the door and grabs my hand in his.

"I want you to really understand," he says in a stern tone, staring me dead in the eyes. "None of those girls matter to me, Valentina."

I still love when he says my name like that. I stroke his big hand.

"I think I get it." He's worried about the compromising position I found him in, worried that I doubt how he feels. "And thank you. Now can we get some dinner and then go back to your place?"

"Of course. Rich is gone for the whole weekend, so we have the apartment to ourselves."

It's been getting trickier and trickier, coming up with excuses to tell my friends for why I've been gone all the time—and why Banon is always the one picking me up. One day, the story was that we were going to help my parents hang up Christmas lights. Another was picking out a Christmas tree. Then seeing Banon's game, which was technically true, but did earn some questions about why I now suddenly cared about seeing him play when I'd talked a lot of shit about him before.

But it'll be Christmas break soon, and then it will get even trickier to keep it a secret from Marissa and my dad. Banon will keep working and living at his apartment, but I'll be staying at their place until school starts up again in January. It's going to look super suspicious if Banon and I are together all the time after spending the last few years barely acknowledging each other.

I sure hate that we have to keep this a secret. I said it would all be fine, that I could handle it if it meant we got to have the relationship that we want—but it's going to be a long break without getting to hook up two or three times a week.

The first time Banon comes to visit for the evening, we go on a long "walk" together to enjoy the fresh snow. Marissa makes sure we're both wearing scarves before sending us off. The first thing we do is scurry to the park, then Banon grabs my hand and leads me off-road. He's not wearing boots—given the hooves and fur and all—and it's fairly deep.

"Don't you get cold?" I ask, gesturing to his feet.

"Me? No." He snorts. "I don't have delicate little toesies like *some* people." He tickles me, making me squeal and giggle. Then his arms loop around my back, bringing me in close to his jacket.

"But you get cold up here," I say, fluffing the scarf around his neck. Marissa loves giving us scarves, even though we only ever wear them at her house.

"Well, that's where my heart is." He traps my hand against his chest, then brings it down to press it to the right side. "Gotta protect that so I can love you with it."

Sometimes Banon is a total cheeseball like

this, and I adore it beyond reason. I didn't know he had this side—a side that wasn't all bluster and arrogance—and it grows on me more every day.

When we part, he tips my chin up, leans down, and brushes his lips over mine.

"I was thinking about fucking you right out here in the woods," he says.

"In a park?!"

"It's after dark, we're off the beaten path…" His hand coasts down over my ass and squeezes it. "You know how to be quiet."

"But it's a public place," I hiss.

"Even more exciting." He releases me and grabs my hand. "Come on, let's go a little farther."

We walk a bit longer through the snow, and I forgot how huge this park was. We came here when I was younger sometimes, because there's workout equipment along the walking path where Banon liked to show off. Never thought we'd be walking through it together, hand in hand.

"Here we go." Banon stops at the trunk of a tall tree. "Keep your coat on, should be fine."

"What should be fine?" I ask quizzically, wondering what he has planned for this tree.

"Pants," he says, and I realize what he's up to.

He was right, and the bark doesn't scratch my back with the big coat on. I manage to keep my cries quiet as he fucks me relentlessly against the tree, groaning as I get closer and closer.

"Yes, Valentina. Come apart." He grunts as I coast right into my orgasm, and the two big hands holding up my ass dig in. "Fuck, you feel so good. I'm going to soak you."

When we're finished, I use some wadded-up tissues in my pocket to clean up, then dump them in the trash when we get back to the path.

A few days after that, I tell Dad and Marissa that Banon and I are going to see a movie. This is code for: fucking at his place.

"Oh, which movie?"

I had this prepared. "That new Deshannon film." I even looked up when it was playing. "At four thirty."

"Can we come?" Marissa says, hopping off the kitchen stool. "I've been wanting to see that."

Great.

Now Banon and I have to sit on opposite

sides of Dad and Marissa during a movie we never intended to see.

I have blue balls, big time. I remembered to bring my sex toys with me, at least, so I can try to imagine Banon's there with me, that massive bull cock of his sunk deep inside me.

I had to size up my dildo.

It feels like it's been eons when Christmas Eve finally rolls around. Banon has an excuse to spend the night because we're all going to drink lots of eggnog and sing songs and watch stupid Christmas movies.

"It's nice seeing you and Banon getting along better," Marissa says while we wait for him to show up. "I'm glad you two got past whatever was going on at Thanksgiving."

Right. That.

"Yeah, we did work through something, I think." My face must be turning red while I lie to her. I've never been a great liar. "Hey, should we check on that casserole? I can smell something burning."

Marissa scurries back to the kitchen just as the front door opens. When I see Banon, all seven feet of pure muscle that he is, I want to throw myself into his arms. I want to drag him back to my bedroom and have my way with him.

Instead, we give a cursory, loose greeting hug. But while his head is lowered, his arm around me, he murmurs, "My room, tonight. Quiet is the word."

Oh, I can do that.

"Quiet is the word," I echo. Then we part, and the parents come out to say hello.

As the sun sets, snow begins to fall outside in big, fat flakes. We all crowd at the window, sipping our eggnog as it covers the front walkway. Then it's time for our annual viewing of all our favorite Christmas films while the ham cooks.

I want to sit beside Banon on the couch, curl up against him with his arm wrapped around me. Instead, I sit on the far end while he takes the La-Z-Boy. I'll glance over at him and find him already looking at me, and then one of us winks or grins before we both try to look away again.

Then the food is out, and it's like Thanksgiving: Volume Two as we dish up potatoes and gravy and crescent rolls. Banon talks about the game he played before Christmas break, and how they won by a big margin. Now his coach is talking about making him captain.

"He caught the most insane throw," I say proudly. "Like, it should have been physically impossible for him to get that ball, and yet."

Banon stares at me, his mouth falling open.

Oh, fuck. I did not mean to say that.

"You saw him play?" Marissa asks, surprised. "I didn't think you went to any of the games, Val."

"Um." I have to think fast to come up with a story. "Yeah. I, uh, wanted to interview him. For the school paper."

Dad raises an eyebrow. "I didn't know you'd joined the newspaper, either."

"Just on a part-time basis. He's an alumnus, you know, so we're always interested in what alumni are doing after they graduate school."

"Working for The Moving Brothers?" Dad asks. "Sounds riveting."

Marissa frowns and elbows him. "Hey, it's a good job."

"Not really newsworthy, though."

"The fact Banon is still playing is newsworthy," I argue. "And doing great for his team, too."

Now both my dad and Marissa are eyeing me with suspicion, while Banon shakes his head on the other side of the table.

"Well, I'm glad you went," his mother finally says. "And it's cool you're on the newspaper now, Val! Exciting stuff."

Great. They're going to want to see the article when it comes out, and there won't be one. Banon sighs, and I wish I'd thought it through just a little more before opening my mouth.

The conversation turns to other things as we stuff our faces. When dinner's over, us kids take up cleaning duty, and I put the leftovers away while Banon starts scrubbing dishes. Once Marissa and Dad go into the living room to set up the next movie, Banon walks past me and grabs my ass on the way.

I shiver all over just thinking about what comes later.

We sit through one more film, this time one of Marissa's favorites, an animated movie with haunting music. It's beautiful and strange, and I'm emotional by the end. When I look over, though, my dad is asleep and Marissa is crying. Banon is watching me, tipping his head.

"That one's intense, isn't it?" he asks. "For being animated."

At last, it's time for bed. We put cookies and milk on the counter and make sure the fire is out, just like when I was a kid. It's a stupid tradi-tion, but it brings all of us joy, and then Dad al-ways eats the cookies in the morning before breakfast, much to Marissa's chagrin.

Then Marissa hands out the packages containing our pajamas—we get a new set every year on Christmas Eve. This time, mine are black and red, with cute little bows on the collar and waist. Banon's are gray and loose fitting, with a slogan across the front that reads, "Mess with the bull and you'll get the horns."

The snow has already piled high in front of the windows, which means a morning of digging out the driveway. But that's for tomorrow me to deal with. For tonight, I can enjoy the soft glow of snowflakes falling under the streetlights as we all stand looking outside. I'm beside Banon by coincidence, and I lightly brush a hand over his thigh to let him know I'm there.

Finally, we turn all the lights off and retreat to our bedrooms. I putter around, trying to read a book for a few minutes before getting impatient with it and tossing it aside. I know I should wait at least an hour for Dad and Marissa to get ready for bed and fall asleep, but I'm anxious to be with Banon again for the first time since that walk in the park.

After wasting more time scrolling on my phone, it's finally late enough that I think we're safe. I head into the Jack-and-Jill bathroom, where Banon's light is still on under his door. I knock quietly, and the low music pauses. Then the door opens, and there's my minotaur again, his black horns gleaming in the light, his nostrils flared as he sniffs me, his blue eyes bright and twinkling. I reach up and run a hand through the buckskin fur along his cheek, leaning into just how soft and warm he is under my fingers.

"Valentina." His tongue licks my name. "You made it."

"Of course I did." I slide into the room, and he closes the door behind me. "Sorry about the newspaper thing. God, that was so stupid."

He grins a sort of sad grin. "Yeah. It was pretty stupid."

We both laugh, then cover our mouths, remembering we need to keep our voices down.

"Quiet's the word," we both say at once.

Banon's arm snakes out and wraps around me, bringing me in against his chest. I love just touching him here, running my fingers over the bulges of his pecs, across his broad shoulders and killer delts.

"I've been in the gym even more since I couldn't see you," he says, one of his muscles flexing under my hand. "Working off all my frustration and hormones."

I quirk a brow. "Hormones?"

He grabs my hands in his and looks me

square in the eye. "Oh, yeah. Minotaur stuff, you know. My hormones have gone crazy since I started having sex with you. My body is obsessed. Can't get enough." He rubs his hips lightly against mine to show off how he's already getting thick and hard for me under his soft sweatpants. "It knows that you're mine. You're all mine, now and always."

I love how that sounds—being with Banon forever, getting to do this every day and night. What a dream that would be, even if we had to keep it secret.

Though that part does suck.

I try not to think about it as Banon leans down to nuzzle my hair. He holds me like I'm something precious, something fragile and also beloved. His big hand skims down my back, over my butt, which he uses to press our bodies closer together.

"Take off your shirt," he rumbles. "Right now."

I do as I'm told, backing away just enough that I can slip my hands under my pajama top. I've got no bra on underneath, so the moment it's on the floor, Banon's eyes drop to my chest. He licks his lips as he cups my breasts in his broad palms, lifting and squeezing and running his fingers over my taut nipples. It's chilly in here with the snow falling outside, and goosebumps spread across my exposed skin.

"Let's get you under the blankets," Banon says, easily sweeping me up into his arms. I squeak and wrap my arms around his neck, and he laughs as he carries me to the bed. "There's a lot I want to do to you there."

CHAPTER
ELEVEN

VALENTINA

Once we're both under the comforter, Banon and I are all over each other—hands and mouths everywhere at once, my leg slinging over his hip to bring him in closer and rub his big dick against my pelvis. He groans at the pressure, and I love how vocal he is with me, that he doesn't mind showing me just how much I please him and how good I feel.

Fingers dip under the band of my pajama pants and then slip into my underwear. Banon's hand is like a heat-seeking missile as he glides to where I'm already growing wetter for him, dipping his biggest finger inside to test me.

"You're going to feel so good," Banon says in a low voice. "All wet for me."

Of course, those words get me going even more. Now he's rubbing that finger over my clit, using my own slick as lube, anchoring me to him with his other arm around my ass. When I twitch and moan, he holds me tighter against him, keeping me trapped as he fingers me.

"It's been too long. I need to lick that pussy."

I gasp in indignation as his hand retreats. But then Banon grabs my pajama pants by the waistband and shoves them down, and I wriggle them off my legs.

"There we go." He rolls us over so he's on top. Lifting up the blanket over his head, he shimmies downward until he's completely hidden, and I can feel his hot, heavy breaths between my legs. "So you don't get cold."

I giggle as he spreads my thighs, and without any pomp or circumstance, he dives in.

Fuck, I'll never get tired of his wide tongue, those talented lips as they suck, those fingers pushing inside me and then petting me until I'm thrashing and holding in my moans. He's so good at this, he really should get a medal.

"Banon, damn," I whimper as I grip his horns under the blanket. He must be getting hot down there, but I only have a quarter of a brain to think about it as sheer bliss takes over me. "Right there, right there."

"Oh, I know," Banon murmurs, his hand speeding up as I get closer and closer. His tongue is doing all sorts of miraculous things, and it's only another few seconds until I'm lost to it, tumbling through the ether, seeing God and all that other stuff they talk about.

I want to get my hand around Banon's cock next, but when he rises from the blankets, his big muzzle glistening, he grabs my wrists and pins me to the bed. When I start to object, he pushes me down more insistently.

"Stay put," he growls. I like when he's horny enough to be bossy, so I remain still as he reaches down and kicks off his own pajama pants. Then his dick is between us again, slobbering against my thigh. Banon kisses me brusquely, conquering my mouth, and I know I'm at his mercy tonight. We've fucked in all kinds of ways, but I think my favorite is still old-fashioned missionary, just because I like to feel his big body on top of mine, weighing me down to the mattress. Sometimes he keeps me pinned like this, using my body until I can't help breaking around him.

"Goddamn, I can't wait to be inside you." Banon nuzzles my hair as he places himself between my legs, lifting my thighs to expose me to him fully. He licks his chops and palms his cock, sliding the head in between my layers until he's softly nudging at my entrance.

It's clearly been a while. He had no trouble fitting last time we had sex, but now he can only push in a hair's breadth before my body resists.

"So small," Banon murmurs affectionately. He keeps his hand wrapped around himself as he tries again, then again, going easy and slow. But I don't want easy and slow. I want fast and hard, even though I know we can't make his bed rattle or risk waking up the rest of the house.

"More," I whisper. "Give me more."

"Are you ready?" he asks, genuine concern in his voice. "It's been a while, and I barely fit as it is—"

"Fuck me. *Please*."

Banon gulps, then nods in a harsh, jerky motion.

"Whatever my woman wants..."

I gasp as he wades in deep in one thrust, demanding that I spread for him, insisting on my body making room. It feels uncomfortable at first, having so much inside me and so suddenly, but I'm slick from my orgasm and tighter than usual.

"...my woman gets." A moan escapes between Banon's clenched teeth as he sinks as far in as he can, breathing hard through his big, flared nostrils. "So tight, fuck. I'm close, Valentina."

Already? We've only just started. Banon's hand clenches around my hip.

"Don't move." He closes his eyes, breathing hard like he's trying to wrestle back control of himself. "I can feel it every time you breathe. Every time your heart beats." His eyes open again, and I marvel in the infinite blue of them, like the ocean. He cradles my face, running his thumb over my cheekbone. "You're so beautiful, I almost can't take it."

I know what he means, especially when he's wearing everything he feels right out there on his sleeve. Nobody could be more handsome.

"And I'm all yours," I say, putting my hand over his.

His smile spreads, familiar and arrogant. "Yes, you are." Slowly he reels his hips back, which makes me yearn and ache to have him again. "Just like I'm yours."

Once more, he jerks his hips forward, stuffing his cock inside me so obscenely that I can't help a cry from escaping. He covers my mouth, muffling me as he slides back, then repeats the motion.

Fuck, I hope I didn't wake them up.

Keeping a tighter lid on myself, I bite my lip as Banon sets a blistering, brutal pace, his muscular thighs flexing with every thrust, his abs tensing and releasing as he fills me up as much as I can bear. He's stimulating everything, the fur on his groin brushing over my clit, his balls hitting my ass as he tucks a hand under my hips and tilts me upward. This way he can get better leverage, and he grunts as our angle changes.

I'm a goner now. He knows I love this, and he uses his powers relentlessly. Soon I'm doing everything I can not to make a sound as my spine tenses, my whole body starting to crumble as pleasure takes me over. I moan against my closed lips, and Banon mutters, "Yes, baby, yes. Give me everything, Valentina. All of it."

As if on command, I break. It's like a bomb has gone off inside me, a sonic blast that ripples through every last nerve ending in my body. I whimper as Banon keeps going, keeps fucking me through it, his grunts and groans of pleasure rising as he hits his own peak. I cover his mouth with my hand as his eyes get wide, and I sense him grow even thicker inside me.

His orgasm is so powerful, he jerks hard, hips driving him deep as he shoots off. I feel warm, so warm, as he fills me up fuller, and it coats my ass as he thrusts in again.

"Fuck," Banon mutters. "I can't stop coming. You just... The way you squeeze me, I can't—"

One last time, he spasms inside me, and then nearly collapses. Managing to hold himself up with one arm, Banon pants, his hot breaths gusting across my face.

"Thank you." He pulls me in close, rolling over onto our sides while he's still buried inside me. "Thank you so much."

"I should be thanking you for all the orgasms."

Banon snorts. "Everything in my life was just practice for you."

I feel all the warm fuzzies as he kisses my neck, then slowly extricates himself from my body. We clean up with the tissues in his drawer, suspiciously placed there beside some lotion.

"Beat it off to the thought of you a lot when I lived in this room," he says by way of explanation.

"Well, I had to upgrade to a bigger dildo. That's how I've been coping."

A snort of quiet laughter bursts out of him, and he throws his arms around me, taking both of us down to the bed.

"I love you, Valentina," he whispers to me, kissing all along the side of my face. "More than I've ever loved anyone. I don't think I even knew love until now."

"I know what you mean." I push some of his rogue shaggy hair away from his eyes. "What are we going to do about it?"

His brows crease. "What do you mean?"

"Are we going to..." I swallow, because I hadn't intended to bring up this subject—but it's been in the back of my mind since break started. "Are we going to tell them?"

Banon frowns. "Of course not."

He says it so quickly, so confidently, that I'm stalled out. It's not even a question in his mind.

"Oh." I try not to let it show that this hurts. I thought it would bother him, keeping this a secret, like it bothers me.

"Imagine what they would do. What they would *say*." He takes both my hands in his, leaning back to really look me in the eyes. "They might disown us, never speak to us again. I couldn't lose my mom like that."

"Dad wouldn't." I don't think he would, at least. I've made mistakes in my life, and he always forgave me. He was fine when he learned I was bisexual, and even encouraged me when I brought a girl home for spring break. He's open-minded and he loves me. "Though he might stop paying for my school."

"Mom might not be so easy. I don't know. I don't *want* to know. I can't stand the idea of what it would do to them if we came clean." He runs a hand through his hair, sitting upright in bed. "Why? Are you thinking of telling them?"

I shake my head as I sit up, too. "Not without you. I would never."

He lets out a *phew*. "Good."

So he's fine with it. He's fine with this being our secret forever. We'll have to live our entire lives under the radar, hoping no one catches on.

I swallow, trying not to get emotional at the idea of existing this way until we're old and our family dies. We just had mind-blowing sex, and I know my brain is going wild with chemicals. Instead, I feign a smile.

"Well, I should get back to my room now."

Banon's brows rise. I'm trying to keep myself

from crying, so I silently get up and make my way over to the door.

"I'm sorry, Valentina." Banon's voice stops me. "I would understand if you don't want this. If you don't want me. Because I know it kills you, keeping a secret. And it kills me, too."

I don't answer because I can't. Tears pool in my eyes as I head into the bathroom, then I close the door of my own bedroom behind me. After staring around at all the posters on my wall, I fall onto the bed.

I should never have done this, because now that I have Banon, I can't possibly let him go.

CHAPTER
TWELVE

BANON

You love your stepsister, you fucking idiot.

I stare in the mirror the next morning, looking bedraggled. I slept like shit without Val at my side. She was supposed to be there with me, but she wasn't. She never will be, not unless I get my own place—which I can't afford.

I've already been here once, trying to find the right way out that doesn't involve giving her up. I would never, *could* never.

I'm so obsessed with my thoughts that as the others wake up on Christmas morning, I've completely forgotten what I put under the tree. Instead, I pretend to be lively and cheery, as one should be. I help make breakfast and say a bright "Good morning" when Val emerges from her room.

She sighs and says, "Hey," before seating herself at the table. She avoids looking at me.

Damn. It's another week until she goes back to school, and then we can really sit down and talk. There must be some kind of road forward out of this where I don't have to hurt her or risk the destruction of my relationship with Mom.

What would she think if she knew? Val is so much younger than I am, even though she acts older. Mom would be disgusted.

I wrinkle my nose like I tasted something bad, and Fred asks if there's shell in the eggs.

Then it's time for presents. To this day, even though we aren't kids anymore, Mom and Fred still like to fill up the space under the tree with gifts. It's mostly silly stuff like socks and underwear, but there are thoughtful, joyful gifts, too. Mom and Fred got me a balance board for working out at home while I'm watching television, claiming it'll give me "killer thighs." Valentina smiles and opens her mouth to crack a joke, then stops herself and turns her head away, her lips twisting.

I wonder what she was going to say.

After another pass around the circle, I open a gift from Val. It's a sweatshirt from our college. Exactly the sort of gift a stepsister gets for her stepbrother. Normal. Not romantic at all.

Then, Valentina picks up a small wrapped box with her name on it.

Oh, fuck.

I meant to give that to her last night, when we were alone. But I set it under the tree and completely forgot to grab it when she came to my room.

Fuckety fuck fuck.

Curious, Val reads the tag and then glances up at me. I can't really snatch it away from her now, or I would look extra ridiculous. I had it wrapped at the store where I bought it, so it's got real fancy gold and red paper and an elaborate bow. Everyone watches as Valentina peels the tape carefully, trying to save the adorable paper—even though it's just going to get recycled anyway—revealing a long, flat, black box.

Her eyes dart up to mine again, this time, confused. I shake my head and drop it into my hands as she opens the box.

"Oh, wow," she breathes. My mom and her

dad both lean forward to get a better look as she takes off the lid. "Thank you, Banon."

Inside is the silver necklace I bought, the one I meant to give her last night. A shining, bright red ruby cut in a pendant shape hangs from the chain—simple and yet elegant, the kind of jewelry that is both a statement piece and will match most of what she wears.

Her dad is the first person to break the silence. He whistles as he takes the box from her to get a better look.

"Wow," he says, glancing down at the velvet bed where the necklace is held in place, then back up at me. "This is real nice."

I don't even know what to say. I wish I could get swallowed up by the earth. It couldn't be more obvious now that I've got feelings of some kind for Val, after giving her something like this in front of everyone.

"Yep, well, I thought Val, uh, deserved something nice."

Fred chuckles. "You're right. It's a beautiful gift."

I don't have the heart to look at my mother. My stepdad is oblivious, yes, but I know she's not so simple to fool. But she doesn't say anything as Val takes the necklace out of the box, admiring it, while casting me looks that say, *What the hell?*

Instead, Mom says, "Let me put it on you, honey," in a gentle, motherly voice. Val kneels in front of the couch. The much larger minotaur delicately takes the necklace, opening the clasp to hang it from Val's neck. Then she reconnects it, and Val lets her dark hair back down.

"Turn around?" Mom asks, and Val obeys, rising to her feet. The ruby pendant hangs down just above the indent between her breasts. It's almost indecent, the way it highlights the soft mounds that are visible, the deep red of the ruby like wine or blood.

"It's beautiful on you, Val." Mom turns to me, and to my surprise, her eyes are soft. "A wonderful gift, Banon."

I gnash my teeth together. Why does it feel like she knows something but isn't willing to say it?

Because she's daring me. She knows my secret, *our* secret, and she's daring me to tell her the truth.

Val is watching us, her expression growing more worried.

"Yeah, it is wonderful," Val echoes. "Thanks

again." She tries to sound light and airy, but I know she's uneasy.

But the rest of the presents go normally, and no one questions either of us any further about the necklace. Together, we make Christmas dinner—which is yet another massive production—and all of us are exhausted by the end of it.

Still, afterward, my mother asks me, "Do you want to go on a walk with me, kiddo?"

Val sits up, glancing between us like she's waiting to be invited, but the invitation never comes.

I nod and swallow. "Yeah, sure."

It feels like I'm signing my own death warrant as we put on our scarves and then head out into the snow, leaving Val and Fred behind to take care of the dishes. I shove my hands in my pockets, hoping Mom's not about to ask me what I think she's going to ask me.

Instead, we both walk in silence along the path around the neighborhood, which must have gotten plowed this morning. Despite it being Christmas, some plow guy was out working.

Plow guy never gets a break.

"Banon," Mom says at last, shattering the silence of the snow around us. "Do you love Valentina?"

I practically choke. I knew something like this was coming, but that wasn't the precise iteration I expected.

"Um, how do you mean?"

"I mean, are you two just messing around, or do you *love* her?"

Fuck. I knew she was on to me. Fuck, fuck, fuck.

"I heard you last night when I went to the bathroom," Mom says. "I always knew when you had a girl over in high school, too. That creaky bed gives you away."

Damn it. I could barely hear it. Stupid super mom ears.

"I just want to know," she continues, "if it's for real, if it's something I need to think about, or if this is a phase."

The answer comes out before I really think it through. "It's not a phase."

She nods.

I barrel onward. "I do love her. Fuck, I love her. I love her so much that it physically pains me. So much that when I look at her, I see everything, all the things I want but can't have."

Her brows rise. "And why can't you have them?"

"You're not... horrified?"

My mother lets out a world-weary sigh. "No, I'm not. I'm disappointed that you two have been keeping secrets. How long has it been going on?"

"Since Thanksgiving. But also... since long before that." God, it's awful to admit. "I've probably loved her for years."

There, I finally said it out loud.

"And she feels the same way?" Mom asks, still gentle and non-judgmental.

I nod. "I think so. She says she does."

"Hmm." She puts her hands in her pockets as we walk, her breath coming out steamy in the cold night air. "Fred won't take it as well."

I shake my head sadly. "I didn't think he would."

"But I can break it to him. I just wish you had come and told me the truth sooner."

I nod, ashamed. I know I should have, too. "I'm sorry. I was afraid of what you'd think."

"You two won't have it easy." She turns to me, stopping in the middle of the path. I stop, too, as she pats my face. "People will always judge you when they learn your story."

"I know." I set my jaw. "But I want Valentina more. And I don't care what they think."

Mom smiles and resumes walking. "That's my boy."

After promising to talk to Fred, we get back to the house and I pack up my things to head home. I have to work over the week between the holidays, as some silly people are still moving this time of year, but I'll be back to pick up Val for a big New Year's Eve party.

I get a text from her, though, the very next day.

Dad knows. Your mom must have told him.

Damn it. I wanted a chance to talk to him myself.

Fuck! Is he mad?

Yes. No. Yes and no.

I don't like the sound of that.

Only a few minutes later, I get a call from Fred himself. When I answer the phone, I say, "Hi, Fred."

"Come over, Banon. For dinner. Right now."

"All right." I don't even try to argue with him. It's time to face the music.

I dress in something nicer, brush my wild hair, and then hop in the car. I'm shaking all the way over to the parents' house, wondering what Fred's going to say to me. I've only seen him really, truly angry once, when someone hit Marissa's car and drove off. She got whiplash in the accident, and they never found the driver.

I swallow hard when I pull up outside, but I have to remember what this is for: a life with Valentina. A life having the person I love closest to me and getting to love her out in the open.

It wasn't in the plan, but it had to happen eventually.

When I come inside, Val is sitting at the table, her dad across from her, my mother on the opposite side from him. Val has tears in her eyes.

She waves a sad greeting as I head to the table and take the fourth seat without being asked. Fred watches me, brows lowered over his eyes, and he is definitely pissed.

"I hear that the two of you have been in a

relationship behind our backs," he says, diving right in. He's just like his daughter. "I also hear that it's rather serious."

I nod. "I love her."

His brows lift. "So she said. It's true, then." He glances between us, his eyes searching. "Is it... is it *get married* type of serious?"

I'm startled by this question. Valentina is young, just turned twenty-one. But I know my answer.

"I would marry her in a heartbeat," I say without hesitating. "But I would want to give her the chance to see more of the world first."

He seems surprised, but pleasantly so, by my answer. He turns to Val.

"Is that how you feel?"

"Oh, yes. But I think I'd rather get married first and then explore the world together." She grins. "I don't want to rush you, though."

My heart soars just hearing these words. That she loves me so much she would be mine, truly, forever.

"No need for all that," Fred says gruffly, re-taking my attention. "I just want to get a measure on where we're at. But I understand now."

Then he lets out a world-weary sigh.

"Dinner's almost ready," he says, getting out

of his chair. "Then we're going to talk some ground rules."

He's not going to disown me? Banish me from the house forever? Even Val has a slight, hopeful smile on her face as he heads to the oven to pull out the pizza he's been cooking.

"Don't get excited," he says as he cuts it up. "It's from that take-and-bake place."

Once we all have our food, Fred lays out his expectations: no sex in his house at all until we're married. He asks us to wait a couple of years before going that far, but if we decide to do it, he'll help us pay for it. He warns us that the world, and probably our extended family, will be less accepting, but we knew that.

Then he asks us if the pizza is any good because we've both been totally silent, and we erupt into a chorus of "It's delicious!"

That night, though, when I head home, I hug Val long and hard, burying my muzzle in her hair. It feels good to not have to hide it, how I feel about her.

"I'll see you when you get back to school," I say, and she nods vigorously.

"I love you," she whispers.

"I love you, too."

EPILOGUE

VALENTINA

Are we getting married only eighteen months later because we absolutely adore each other and know we want to be together forever? Yes.

Is it a little bit so that we're allowed to sleep in the same bedroom at our parents' house? Also yes.

Some of our friends weren't so understanding, but most of them came around to it. It was tougher to convince Rich, but ultimately he's Banon's best friend and wants the best for him. My buddies at college have all supported me, and I'm more than grateful. I graduated two months ago, and now I'm knee-deep in my summer internship doing data analysis. Banon has moved to football full-time, playing for his team as the new captain and coaching teens when he's not playing. He plans to move all the way into coaching in a few years, when his time on the field is over.

Dad has agreed to walk me down the aisle, though some of the extended family refused to attend the ceremony. The cousins and uncles and aunts who are here, though, have plenty of awkward questions for us.

I just want to get this all over with so we can finally be alone later tonight.

I haven't laid eyes on Banon since yesterday, and I can't wait for him to see my dress. It's *not* white, thank you very much. It's black and red, with black lace detailing, and my silver and ruby pendant hanging from my neck. I look very much like an evil queen, and it's exactly how I imagined myself getting married.

Banon's waiting for me at the altar in a black suit with a red shirt and bowtie, so we match perfectly. One of my bridesmaids waits to hold my flowers as I come down the aisle, Dad's arm wrapped around mine.

He's come around to it, too, as time has gone

on. He sees the way Banon keeps me close during movies, helps me cook dinner, holds my hand on family walks, and treats me with all the love and kindness in his big heart.

Especially the cheesy, lovey-dovey shit he says to me that gives my own dad's dad jokes a run for their money.

I don't even notice the altar or the flowers hanging from it as I approach my husband-to-be. Damn, he is so fine in that tuxedo, filling it out as far as it can possibly stand. He's huge and broad and perfectly, wonderfully mine.

Banon holds out his hand to me, and I take it as Dad lets me go.

"I love you, honey," Dad says as he takes his seat next to Marissa in the front row.

"I love you too, Dad."

Then it's time. I look into Banon's blue eyes as the officiant speaks, and I barely hear anything she's saying because I'm that deep in them. He smiles so affectionately, with so much love worn right on his sleeve, that I feel like I might cry.

This big minotaur loves *me*.

Then he says his vows, and they might just be the most beautiful words possible, hearing every small thing he loves about me, from my fashion sense to my fake newspaper story. I cringe at that. He imagines our future lives together and all the joy we'll find in it together. The pets we'll have, and maybe the kids we'll adopt someday.

By the time it's my turn, I can barely speak through my tears. But I manage to say my own vows from memory, how I'm only complete because Banon is here with me. How he's everything I dreamed of having for myself and more.

And then, the audience claps, and he kisses me. My minotaur wraps me up and bends me back as he conquers my lips, showing his love to me for all the world to see.

THANK YOU FOR READING!

I hope you enjoyed Banon and Valentina's story. If you did, please consider leaving a review! Reviews are incredibly helpful to indie authors like me in finding new readers.

JOIN MY NEWSLETTER!

For all the latest regarding books, and to get access to a FREE novella, join my newsletter!

www.LyonneRiley.com

Get lots of steamy art to go with your favorite stories! Visit me on Patreon for my latest ongoing serial.

Patreon.com/LyonneRiley

ABOUT THE AUTHOR

Lyonne Riley published her first book at age five, which was written on tiny sheets of notebook paper, and she insisted on giving a copy to everyone she knew. She's been writing ever since, from fan fiction in her teen years to original fiction as an adult. After a stint in traditional publishing, she discovered what she truly wanted to write: very smutty stories about monsters and the little humans they worship.

Now she lives in the middle of nowhere with her dogs and spouse, writing sexy fairy tales.

ACKNOWLEDGMENTS

I would like to thank everyone involved in helping me through the process of putting out this book. I can't say enough how much I appreciate the help and encouragement of the people around me—especially Amber, who told me I could do this in the first place.

Huge thank you to Rowan Woodcock for the gorgeous cover illustration. A big thank you to Ana Hansen of Sparks Editorial for reading my little book in one day (!!). To my critique partners, who gave me phenomenal feedback: You all make this possible. And of course, my amazing spouse, who has always supported my dreams—and given me lots of inspiration for my characters' sexy adventures.

I couldn't have done this without the expertise of my fellow self-published romance authors. Thank you for inviting me into your circles and helping me through this process.

And thank you to my readers, who gave this book a shot.